Last Dance, Second Chance

ALSO BY EMMA BENNET

HER PERFECT HERO
THE GREEN HILLS OF HOME
THE ONE THAT GOT AWAY?
STARSTRUCK
FALLING IN LOVE AT NIGHTINGALE FARM
A CHRISTMAS TRUCE
THE BABY PLAN
LAST DANCE, SECOND CHANCE

last dance, second chance

Emma Bennet

JOFFE BOOKS

Joffe Books, London
www.joffebooks.com

First published in Great Britain in 2024

Cover art by The Brewster Project

ISBN: 978-1-83526-693-9

This one's dedicated to my princes,
Hector and Paris.
Thank you for the love and chaos,
my beautiful furry boys. xx

CHAPTER ONE

Every muscle in Jessica's 31-year-old body ached, as they did every morning. She groaned as she forced herself out of bed — she might be a proud member of the 5 a.m. club, but that didn't mean she had to enjoy the actual execution of it. She wasn't sure she'd ever get fully used to waking up when it was still dark outside.

Her apartment didn't seem to have cooled down at all during the night, despite her keeping the windows wide open. The constant noise from the street below was slightly preferable to the stifling heat with them closed. New York in an August heatwave was no joke, especially when you'd grown up with British summers. Maybe one day she'd live somewhere with air con.

A cool shower helped to revive her somewhat, and she dressed in her leotard, adding a pair of shorts and a loose vest top. There was no point in make-up — she'd soon be sweating so much it would just slide off her face. She was lucky that her dark eyelashes and red lips meant she never needed to wear much make-up anyway. She pulled her long jet-black hair into a well-practised chignon and downed a protein shake while packing her bag with her water bottle and a variety of snacks — she didn't usually have much time to eat during the day, so relied heavily on foods that could be consumed quickly and with minimal mess while giving her maximum nutrition.

She was walking down the three flights of stairs from her tiny attic apartment before six, and dawn was breaking.

* * *

The studios of the Greenwich Ballet Company were only a ten-minute walk from Jessica's home, a commute she counted as an extra warm-up ahead of her day of dance practice. The smell of steaming rubbish made Jessica wrinkle her nose, but at least the streets were quieter than they would be later, which she liked. Jessica hummed along to Tchaikovsky's *The Sleeping Beauty* score. She'd rehearsed parts of it so much, it had been playing on a loop in her head for weeks.

The company was still on the annual lay-off period, which meant Jessica had been teaching at a dance summer school, and waiting tables before that, since the company had broken up at the end of May. She had another fortnight before the company would be back full-time, but Jessica and a number of the company's other dancers had returned to training early. They'd had auditions for their next ballet and were now using these couple of weeks to get properly back into shape.

The doors to the ballet company opened at 6 a.m., but the building was quiet, with no classes or rehearsals going on at the moment. Some summer schools would still be running for the rest of the week but didn't start until much later in the day.

Jessica smiled as she stepped inside and the unique smell of dance shoes, wood polish and coffee hit her nostrils. She adored this old building and had ever since she first stepped into its shabby hallways as a nervous eighteen-year-old, thousands of miles away from her family home in England and desperate to prove herself among the polished-looking American girls with their designer leotards and bored-sounding accents. Thirteen years on, and Jessica had more than

2

earned her place as a soloist for the company. A position which had allowed her to travel the world performing in some of the most amazing venues, in Paris, Sydney and London to name just a few. And it was every bit as wonderful as she'd imagined it would be.

She was living the life she'd dreamt about as a teenager in her little bedroom in her parents' semi-detached home in Kent, exhausted and juggling homework with intensive ballet competition and practice. Back then, she'd been terrified she'd grow taller, fill out and not remain five foot four and slim with almost perfect measurements to become a professional ballerina.

Jessica stole a glance at the building's noticeboard as she passed — nothing had been posted on the outcome of their auditions yet. It was hardly surprising because the office wouldn't be open for hours — but announcements were due later that day.

Jessica found empty practice space with ease. There were some dancers in the company who liked to work in a room with others, but Jessica relished the quiet of being by herself in a studio first thing in the morning. She liked to take her time warming her muscles up and to spend as long as she needed working on anything she was struggling with, without having to worry about someone else wanting to move on or getting fed up with her playing the same few bars of music through her little speakers again and again.

Jessica set up her speakers in the corner and selected the music on her phone.

She took off her shorts and top and began working her way through the routines she'd done almost every day of her life since her first ballet class aged five, following every movement her body made in the mirror on the opposite side of the room. First position was so natural to her that it was her standard resting pose — even when waiting in line at the supermarket. She worked her way diligently through the exercises, only stopping to take a sip of water and wipe herself down with a towel — the building was too old for built-in air con, and its huge windows meant it heated up quickly. The large fans placed in each of the studios merely moved the hot air around.

But today Jessica couldn't lose herself in the familiar routines as she usually did. Her gaze repeatedly flitted to the large clock on the wall. It seemed to be moving far slower than usual. She went over to her phone — the clock was right and time was indeed dragging.

Once she'd completed her hour's practice she finished her water, packed up her stuff and went down the corridor and into the gym. She flinched at the change from the quiet and solitude of the studio to the busyness and noise of the people and machines. Dance music blasted out of speakers on the wall and she waved hello to the other dancers already there, working hard. Everyone was keen to show the casting decision-makers just how much effort they put in.

"Hey, Jess," called a brunette running on the treadmill.

"Hiya, Bethany." Jessica walked over to her friend. "Is there any news?" she asked quietly.

"Not that I've heard. The list might not be up until this evening I guess," Bethany whispered back in her Boston accent.

Jessica exhaled. "I'm going to be a mess by then!"

"Let's do our workout and have a quick shower, and then we can go and grab a coffee. I could do with the caffeine hit — and it'll take up another half hour," Bethany suggested.

"That sounds like a good idea."

The friends focused on their gym session, their natural competitiveness leading them to push themselves harder than when they exercised alone — a trait that would ensure they had even sorer muscles than usual the next morning.

* * *

A couple of hours later, Jessica and Bethany returned through the large double doors of the dance company to find a crowd gathered around the noticeboard. They looked at each other, nerves written clearly on both their faces.

"Let's play it cool," Jessica said, trying to ignore the butterflies performing the "Dance of the Sugar Plum Fairy" in her stomach. Bethany nodded. They held back, seemingly checking their phones until the squealing had died down and most of the dancers had moved on.

Without speaking, Jessica and Bethany walked over to the board. "Congratulations!" called out a young dancer Jessica knew only by sight.

"Thanks," Jessica said without thinking, focusing on the piece of paper pinned to the centre of the board with '*Sleeping Beauty Cast Sheet*' typed in large, bold letters at the top. Superstition meant Jessica always began scanning the cast list from the bottom — the smallest roles — up. As her eye travelled further and further up the list without seeing her name, the excitement within her progressively built. Her gaze came to rest on the line right below the list's title: '*Princess Aurora — Jessica Stone*'. A delighted smile broke out across her face.

"I knew you'd get it!" cried Bethany, giving her a hug. "And look, I'm your understudy!"

Bethany was the only real friend Jessica had ever made in the ballet world, and the secret to their friendship seemed to be that they were both at different stages of their careers. At only twenty-three, Bethany didn't have the years of experience Jessica did and had only been a soloist for a year. The pair weren't usually in direct competition with each other. Jessica was able to help and advise her friend, while being kept on her toes by seeing how supple her younger friend's body was, even if her dancing wasn't as precise as Jessica's.

Jessica tried not to think about how Bethany's potential huge chance rested solely on Jessica injuring herself and being unable to dance. After all, it was Jessica who'd been given the opportunity to finally move up to principal ballerina. And the part of Aurora was her absolute favourite in the whole of ballet. It was the role she'd longed to play more than any other since her mother had taken her to see a production of *The Sleeping Beauty* when she was five and Jessica's talent for dancing had made itself apparent.

"I'm going to call my mum. She'll be waiting by the phone — she gets so nervous for me," Bethany said, skipping off.

A pang went through Jessica at the thought of how lovely it would be to have someone waiting by the phone to find out in what role she'd been cast. She hadn't told her own family about the audition — hadn't spoken to them for quite a while, actually, as she'd been busy working and the time difference made calls tricky to schedule. It wasn't that they wouldn't be interested to hear her news — she knew they would, and they'd be pleased for her— but they never seemed to understand how important ballet was to her. And they certainly wouldn't understand how much landing this particular role meant. To them, dancing was just her job, but to her it was everything.

Jessica was too excited and relieved to return to any sort of practice. Of course, it hadn't come as a complete surprise to her that she'd been given the role. She knew how good she was. She never would have continued with ballet, pushed herself so hard to be the best she could, if she hadn't known she was capable of being at the very top of her profession. She couldn't have been happy languishing in the corps. But Jessica had reached the point in her career when she was all too aware that she wouldn't be at the top of her game for that much longer, and she only had a relatively short amount of time to be able to play the principal roles she'd prepared her whole career for. Aurora was a big one to tick off her ballet bucket list.

"I see you're going to be my princess," said a male voice from behind her.

Jessica turned round to face Gabriel, a handsome Portuguese dancer who was set to play her Prince Charming.

"Gabriel, congratulations," she said, kissing him lightly on both his cheeks.

"And to you." He smiled. "Not that anyone doubted your casting. Everyone knew that role would be yours. It's past time for you to be promoted to principal."

Jessica smiled in what she hoped was a suitably modest manner.

"So, I thought you might like to go out with me tonight to celebrate. We could get some dinner, maybe go to a club . . ." He ran his hands through his thick, dark hair.

"Thanks for the offer, Gabriel, but I think I'll pass."

"No problem, beautiful. I guess I'll see you at rehearsals in a couple of weeks if not before." He flashed her a confident grin.

"Yeah, see you then."

She watched Gabriel head off down the corridor, calling out to another dancer ahead of him, and sighed. She'd heard that she'd get a lot more interest from the male dancers once she got her first principal role. She was glad he'd taken her rebuttal so well. Gabriel was a nice guy, and they needed to keep things friendly between them if they were to spend hours every day dancing together over the next few months. It was because of this that Jessica had a policy of never dating other dancers, no matter how sexy their accents might be. This policy, combined with a further rule of never dating non-dancers because they just didn't understand how important her career was to her and how much of her life it took up, meant she didn't date at all. A state she was usually completely happy with, even if it did sometimes leave her feeling lonely on a Saturday night.

* * *

Jessica walked back to her flat. She'd spend a couple of hours there quietly by herself. Tidy up a bit, and allow her heart rate to normalise before returning for more practice later. She'd appear to be that unfazed, polished ballerina she prided herself upon showing to the world.

She loved her little home. It was only a studio but it was cosy and, more importantly, in a rather run-down brownstone, which made her feel like Carrie Bradshaw every time she walked up the stone steps to its front door. Despite this, she didn't spend all that much time in it. She was either at classes, rehearsals or performing, or out in the evening at one of the many events the company held to raise funds. She rarely had visitors and, as a result, her flat was usually a bit of a mess.

Jessica got some multi-purpose cleaner and a cloth from under the sink, and set to work on her kitchen. This was probably the cleanest room in the place as Jessica rarely cooked, being much more likely to pick up something ready-made from the local health food shop on her way home in the evenings. She put some music on, the 'Black Swan' *pas de deux* from *Swan Lake*, and moved around to the melody as she worked, muscle memory meaning she remembered the steps perfectly and had to make herself continue cleaning rather than surrender to the urge for her whole body to join in completely with the dance.

She recalled how pleased Bethany had been to be named her understudy. It wouldn't be many years before her friend would be the one getting the principal roles over herself, and Jessica wondered whether their friendship would survive that. She hoped it would. It was good to have an ally in the dance world and she wouldn't want to go back to being without one. The career she'd chosen could be surprisingly lonely.

Jessica's phone beeped. She picked it up to see a WhatsApp message from her mum, Sarah, with a picture attached of Jessica's youngest niece, Sophie, at a birthday party. She stood in front of a huge cake with a number four candle on top. Bum, Jessica thought. She'd forgotten another birthday. She wished she was the type of person who put reminders in her phone for this sort of thing, but the only reminders she had were for physiotherapy appointments and to record her protein consumption.

She quickly logged in to Amazon and sent a gift certificate for her niece to her brother's email. An e-card would have to do as well.

She looked at the photo again and smiled at how happy Sophie looked. She was getting so big. How long had it been since she'd seen her? Christmas? No, she'd been in *The*

8

Nutcracker over Christmas. It must have been the summer before.

All of a sudden, she had an urge to see her family. Her mum and dad both knew that it had been her dream to dance Aurora since she was tiny. *The Sleeping Beauty* was her favourite ballet, and she had performed in it before, as the Lilac Fairy and as a nymph when she was new to New York and in the corps. She wanted to be able to share her news with her family properly, not just over the phone. She had the next couple of weeks before rehearsals would start . . . Maybe she'd also be able to convince her mum and dad to at least visit her in New York and see her perform.

She quickly checked her bank balance on her banking app. Thanks to how hard she'd been working for the past few months, and the very good tips she received from waitressing, she could just about cover a flight. She could be at her parents' house by tomorrow afternoon and tell them her news. And she could take her niece out for a post-birthday treat. Before she could think better of the amount of money she was spending, Jessica bought herself a return ticket to London Heathrow, departing that night.

CHAPTER TWO

Jessica sighed with happiness as she stepped out of the airport terminal and into the British summer. It was one o'clock in the afternoon and twenty-two degrees Celsius. The perfect antidote to the New York heat.

She gave herself twenty minutes in the sun with a coffee, and then hopped on the Heathrow Express to Paddington before catching the train to Bowerbridge, the little town where her parents as well as her brother, Andrew, and his family lived.

By the time she walked along the road from the train station, Jessica was somewhat regretting her decision to surprise her parents. If they'd known she was arriving, her mum or dad would have insisted upon coming to pick her up from the airport and she wouldn't be dragging her luggage along behind her now. But it would be so lovely to see the excitement on their faces when they opened their front door to find her outside. She hoped they were in. Her dad might be at work — he ran the local estate agent's, and had done for over thirty-five years. Her mum was a teacher at the town's primary school, so she was on summer holidays. If no one was home, Jessica knew where they kept their spare key so she could let herself in and wait for them, or wander down to

10

her dad's office and surprise him there. Her mum sometimes popped in to lend a hand during the holidays so Jessica might find her there too.

She turned the corner into the cul-de-sac. Their cars were in the driveway so that was a good sign. Jessica stood across the street from her family's home for a moment. The house was red brick and perfectly symmetrical at the front, like a doll's house, with a window on either side of the front door, and three windows evenly spaced along the upstairs.

This was the house she'd lived in until she'd moved to America, though she'd been away during term time at dance school in London for two years before that. She'd been so desperate to leave the little town which had no professional ballet academy, so intent upon following her dream — a dream she'd have had to put on hold if she'd stayed at home and taken A levels at the local sixth-form college. Her parents had been amazing, though she knew they missed her terribly.

Jessica took a deep breath and went to cross the road, but stopped when she heard a voice calling, "Jessica Stone, well I never!" She turned and hoped she'd managed to hide the dismay she felt at the sight of the enormous grey-haired figure of Mrs Edith White hurrying along the pavement towards her. Mrs White, as anyone under the age of sixty referred to her, considered herself the matriarch of the town. She'd lived there her whole life and knew everyone, and was on so many committees that Jessica doubted even she remembered all of them. Basically, if you lived in Bowerbridge and wanted to do so much as put new Christmas lights on the tree outside your property, you'd better check with Mrs White first.

"Good afternoon, Mrs White," Jessica said, dutifully.

"So, you've finally been able to manage a visit!" Mrs White proclaimed. "Thank goodness your parents have your brother, is all I can say. I don't know how they'd manage without him."

Jessica's mum and dad were only in their late fifties, and in good health. She knew they didn't rely on her brother to look after them, but that didn't mean Mrs White's words didn't rankle.

"He's a wonderful son," Jessica replied through gritted teeth.

"So, will you be staying for long?" Mrs White asked nosily.

"No. It's just a flying visit. I've got to get back to work."

"Oh, yes. The dancing." She said it like she was sure Jessica was secretly a stripper or a pole dancer.

"That's right. Anyway, lovely to see you again, but I really must go. Mum and Dad are waiting for me," Jessica fibbed.

"Do give them my regards," Mrs White said, and she bustled off down the road.

Jessica would have liked to have taken a few moments to compose herself again — an encounter with Mrs White was always unsettling — but her mum chose that moment to open the front door and come out with a bag of rubbish for the bin. Sarah looked up and spotted her daughter. "Jessica?! What are you doing here, darling?" She dropped the garbage in order to rush to greet her daughter with a hug. Sarah was the same height as Jessica, and slim, but not to ballerina standards. She'd also had black hair, but it was heavily peppered with silver now.

"I wanted to surprise you!" Jessica said, pushing Mrs White firmly to the back of her mind.

"Well, you've certainly done that!"

Jessica spotted a troubled look pass over her mother's face.

"Is everything all right, Mum?" she asked.

"Yes, of course. It's wonderful to see you. It's just . . . well, why don't you come in and see. Let me take your case for you."

Puzzled, Jessica followed her mum through her parents' colourful little front garden and into the house. She was greeted enthusiastically by a large golden retriever.

"Who's this?" Jessica asked, laughing as the dog did its best to lick her anywhere it could.

"This is Monty," Sarah said. "We adopted him a few weeks ago. Your dad saw a photo of him on the local dog rescue's Facebook page and it was love at first sight."

"Wow! I thought you didn't want a dog . . ."

"Your dad wore me down," Sarah admitted. "Monty's going to go into the office with him when I'm back at work. We were going to introduce you to him the next time we FaceTimed."

Jessica looked around her and realised the floor of the hallway was covered in packed suitcases.

Jessica turned to her mum. "What's going on?"

"We're going on holiday," Sarah said. "We're leaving tomorrow morning."

"Oh no!" cried Jessica.

"I'm so sorry, sweetheart. If we'd known you were coming, we never would have booked it."

"It's not your fault. It was all so last-minute. I wanted to surprise you!"

"It was a lovely surprise," said Sarah, pulling her daughter in for another hug. "Your dad's going to be thrilled to see you."

Jessica felt completely deflated. How stupid of her to think she could just turn up and her whole family wouldn't have any plans in the middle of the summer holidays.

"We're going to the Lake District with Andrew, Molly and the kids. We've rented a cabin for ten nights. Maybe we could fit you in as well? It's two bedrooms so Andrew and Molly are going to have Peter in their room and Emily and Sophie are going to sleep on sofa beds in the sitting room. Maybe they could squish on one and you could sleep on the other?"

As much as Jessica wanted to spend some time with her family, ten nights in a tiny cabin with all seven of them, combined with the idea of sharing a room with her two nieces and sleeping on a sofa bed did not really appeal. She was formulating a polite response when the telephone rang.

"Just a minute, love," Sarah said, and she went into the kitchen to answer it.

Jessica stroked Monty absent-mindedly as she looked around her family home. The last time she'd been here, she now remembered, was when she was performing at Sadler's Wells for a couple of weeks and she'd visited her parents for the weekend. The house was still reassuringly very similar to when she'd lived there, though the addition of Monty was a definite surprise. She supposed it had been quite a while since she'd taken the time to check in with her family, and she tended to dissuade them from calling her as she was usually so busy. She could kick herself for not at least ensuring they'd be around during her visit.

Sarah rejoined her. "That was the dog-sitter we had booked — she's ill and can't take Monty while we're away. This is exactly the type of thing I warned would happen if we got a dog!" she said, exasperated. "Your dad was only happy with Monty going to her because he's been taking Monty to visit her house every other day to get him familiar with it and he knows Monty gets on with her dogs. There's no time to get Monty used to another place now and we booked the cabin months and months ago, before Monty, so it didn't bother us that they had a strict no-dog policy."

"Do you think Monty would be happy staying with me here?" Jessica asked.

"You can't stay here by yourself for ten nights!" Sarah said immediately. "The cabins were fully booked before, but maybe they've had a cancellation for a one-bedroom one . . ." Her forehead furrowed.

"I'll be fine," Jessica reassured her. "It will be nice to be able to relax at home and unwind, and I can take Monty for lots of walks. I'll have this evening with you and then a few days when you get back and before I have to leave."

"Andrew and Molly could go by themselves and we could stay with you—"

"I don't want you to miss your holiday, and the kids would be disappointed. They will have been looking forward to going away with you," Jessica reasoned. She really didn't want the family holiday to be cancelled because of her. It wasn't like her mum and dad got away much at all; she was sure they'd have been looking forward to it for months. "And I bet you've promised Andrew and Molly that you'll babysit at least one evening so they can go out together."

"But it's so lovely to have you here! I want to make the most of it!"

Jessica noticed her mum's eyes were wet with unshed tears and put her arm around her. "I know, so do I. But I'm honestly happy to stay with Monty. I'll look after the house — I know how Dad worries about leaving it empty — and then we'll have a great time together when you get back. We can take the children out for the day together, maybe."

"That would be lovely. Are you absolutely sure? It would be a big help having you look after Monty and the house."

"Absolutely, Mum."

"Well, thank you, darling," said Sarah, giving her daughter another hug. "I still can't believe you're here! I must call your dad and tell him!"

"No, don't do that. I'll wander down to the office and surprise him there." Jessica grinned at the thought. She couldn't wait to see her dad.

"He'll love that. Do you want a cup of tea and something to eat before you go?"

"I'm fine, thanks, Mum. I ate on the plane." Jessica reflected that it would take her a while to readjust to the amount of tea drinking that went on in her family home. Her mum never knowingly allowed the kettle to cool down while she was in the house.

"All right, he should be nearly done for the day by the time you get there."

Jessica headed back out again, relishing the gentle warmth of the sun. She must have walked to her dad's estate agency hundreds of times as a child. She used to love to go in and spin on the office chairs and play games on his computer in the back while he talked to prospective clients. She passed by the school her mum taught at and which she had attended until she was eleven. The Victorian building looked just the same, with the original 'boys' and 'girls' entrances and rows of large windows, except that it had a fancy new sign outside. It was a small school, with less than two hundred pupils.

Everyone had known that Mrs Stone, who taught Year 4, was her mum. Having her mother as a teacher for a year hadn't actually been as bad as Jessica had worried it would be. Jessica had behaved, knowing she'd be in trouble when she got home if she didn't, even if her mum wouldn't tell her off properly in front of her schoolmates.

She continued on, and noticed a man of about her age on the other side of the road. A springer spaniel trotted alongside him on a lead. He was speaking into his phone — and was very good-looking. He must have been at least six foot two with short dark hair and the sort of chiselled jaw seen in commercials for shaving foam. The jeans and T-shirt he wore hinted at a strong body underneath. Something about him was familiar. She just wished she could place what it was. He caught her gaze and smiled, a look of semi-recognition passing over his face. Jessica couldn't seem to stop herself from smiling back, but swiftly averted her eyes, embarrassed at being caught staring at a stranger in the street.

A few minutes later, Jessica pushed open the doors to Stone's Property Agency, to the familiar jingle of the bell signalling the arrival of a customer. The office was empty except for her dad, Joe, and Meryl, who was in charge of lettings and had worked in the agency for nearly as long as her father. Joe looked up from his computer and his mouth fell open at the sight of his daughter. "Jessica!" he cried out and rushed over to her. He bent down to hug her. "Have you got smaller?"

"Nope," said Jessica laughing.

"Well, I've got bigger." Joe laughed, rubbing his stomach. Her dad loved cooking and eating, and had indeed become rounder since the last time she'd seen him.

"What on earth are you doing here?" he asked.

"I wanted to surprise you with a visit, but I really should have called ahead first! Mum's filled me in about your holiday."

"Yes . . ."

"Don't worry, Mum and I have got it sorted," she said. "We'll tell you all about it when we get home. Hello, Meryl!"

16

"Hello, Jessica! How lovely to see you. How have you been?"

"I'm good. Is my dad still overworking you?"

"Wouldn't seem right if he wasn't!" Meryl laughed. "Joe, why don't you head off with Jessica? We don't have any more bookings today and I can handle any walk-ins."

"I think I will," said Joe. "Thanks, Meryl."

* * *

An hour later, Jessica and her mum sat at the kitchen table while her dad prepared supper for them all. He'd insisted on popping to the supermarket on the way home to pick up salmon because it was Jessica's favourite, and he knew, while she'd relish a few of the crispy potatoes he'd roast to go alongside, it was salad that would fill most of Jessica's plate. She also didn't join her parents in having a glass of wine, sticking to water instead. She only usually had a small glass of alcohol at functions organised by her company when it would be awkward not to. It affected her dancing performance the next day too much for her to want to drink it any more often.

As Monty slept by her feet, her mum and dad filled her in on all the local gossip. "Oh, and there's a new doctor down at the surgery. He's very nice, even Mrs White approves of him. His family used to live here but moved away. I taught him. Actually, I think he might have been in your class—"

Sarah was interrupted by a ring at the doorbell. "I wonder who that can be?" asked Joe, with a glint in his eye. "Why don't you go and see, Jess?"

Jessica smiled; her dad was so obvious. She went into the hallway, opened the front door and found herself enveloped by her brother, Andrew, his wife, Molly, and their children, Peter, Emily and Sophie.

"Hey, sis! Mum called and told us you were here. Great timing for a visit!" Andrew teased. Andrew was a bear of a man, taller than their father by a good six inches at least, with wild black hair, and a growing belly thanks to his wife's good cooking and his rather sedentary day job as an accountant. "I know. I can't believe it. It's not like they go away a lot!" Jessica replied.

"It's good to see you," Molly said, scooping up little Sophie so she didn't get crushed under everyone. Like her husband, Molly was still wearing the suit she wore to work as a fellow partner in their accountancy firm. She was tall and slim and her blonde hair was in a no-nonsense high ponytail. Jessica imagined Molly could be very serious when it came to business, but when she was with her family, she let all that slide and devoted herself to them completely.

"Come through, come through," called Joe from the kitchen.

Everyone trooped in, the children gazing up at Jessica like she was a world-famous film star.

"We can't stay for long, but we wanted to pop in and say hi to Auntie Jessica, didn't we guys?" said Molly.

"We watched you on the television, Auntie Jessica," Emily, who was six, said, looking up at her auntie with wide eyes. "You were beautiful."

"Thank you," Jessica said, smiling.

"Your company's *The Nutcracker* was on the BBC last Christmas. The girls were completely enamoured," Molly explained.

"I'm glad they enjoyed it." She wished her brother had told her. She'd had no idea they'd watched her performance.

"I'd love to dance like you," whispered Sophie.

"It takes a lot of hard work," Jessica said.

"And doesn't leave a lot of time for anything else," muttered Andrew, which earned him a glare from Sarah. Jessica chose to ignore his comment.

"Anyway, we'd better go," said Molly. "We were just on our way home from picking Peter up from football, and we need to get an early night."

"We're going on holiday with Nanny and Grandad tomorrow, Auntie Jessica," Sophie explained. "Are you coming as well?"

"No. I'm going to look after Monty here, but I'll see you all when you get back."

"I'm glad someone's looking after Monty," Peter said. "I was worried about him."

"He'll be fine with me." Jessica gave him a reassuring smile. She couldn't believe how much the children had grown, especially Peter. At almost eight and a half he'd soon be as tall as his aunt.

Andrew and his family left in a whirlwind, making the kitchen seem quite empty afterwards.

Jessica enjoyed her supper and stayed up as long as she could to chat with her parents but was eventually forced to excuse herself. She was exhausted from travelling and desperate to go to bed.

Climbing up the stairs of her parents' house, hearing her mum and dad chatting away downstairs as they settled down to watch some television together, made her feel like a teenager again. The bathroom seemed strange without her and her brother's toothbrushes next to the sink, and there was a new blind up at the window. Every time she visited there seemed to be something different about her childhood home. But her old bedroom was exactly the same as when she'd lived in the house. She settled into her old single bed underneath a poster from the English National Ballet and fell fast asleep.

CHAPTER THREE

Jessica woke up the next morning to the sounds of her parents moving around downstairs in the kitchen. She checked her phone. It was 10 a.m. — she'd slept for thirteen hours.

She pulled her old dressing gown around her; she'd found it in the wardrobe in the corner of the room — she couldn't believe her parents had kept all of her clothes from when she was a teenager!

The smell of coffee led her downstairs, where she found her mum and dad tidying up. She was greeted enthusiastically by Monty. He certainly didn't act like a dog who'd only met her yesterday!

"Hey, Sleeping Beauty!" said her dad when he saw her.

Her big news came flooding back to her: how could she have omitted to tell her parents? That had been one of the main reasons she'd wanted to come to visit them. It must have been the excitement of seeing everyone combined with how tired she was from travelling.

"I forgot to tell you last night," Jessica said. "I've been given the role of Princess Aurora in my company's new production of *The Sleeping Beauty*. It's my first role as a principal ballerina. Rehearsals start in two weeks."

"Well done, love," said her mum, giving her a hug and placing a large mug of coffee in front of her. "I bet it'll be nice to get back to dancing. This summer break thing is really unfair. You should get paid for your summer holidays like I do."

"It's what all ballet companies do, Mum, not just mine," Jessica replied defensively.

"It just doesn't seem very reasonable to me to expect you all to find alternative employment for months at a time."

"Would you rather I didn't have any off time at all and risked an injury?"

"Of course not!"

"You'll make a brilliant Aurora," her dad intercepted, always the peacemaker.

"I'm sorry I'm down so late. I must have slept through you both getting up." Jessica found she wanted to change the subject. She didn't want to argue with her parents before they left.

"You were exhausted, sweetheart. Did you sleep well?" Sarah asked.

"Like a log," Jessica said, smiling.

"Good to hear," her dad said. "I've written down instructions for feeding Monty. You'll need to watch him because he does still jump up to grab food from the countertops. He's pretty good on the lead now, but he's only one and a half and his recall isn't great, so if you let him off make sure it's in a contained area. There's that bit down the river by the golf club which is perfect for him."

"We'll be fine, Dad," Jessica said, rubbing Monty's ears. It was sweet how her dad fussed over the dog. He'd wanted one, and a golden retriever in particular, for as long as she could remember. Jessica and Andrew had both regularly joined in his entreaties, but her mum had always said no because they were such a commitment. Looking back at her childhood, Jessica could understand why. Her parents had spent a huge amount of their spare time driving her around to dance classes and competitions; trying to fit a dog into that life as well would have been pushing it.

"We'd better be off," Sarah said. "We're going to drive round to Andrew's so that they can fit some of their luggage into my car. It's a bit of a squeeze with the five of them in their Renault as it is."

Jessica helped carry her parents' luggage out to the car for them.

"Have a brilliant time. Make sure you send me loads of pictures," she said as they did up their seatbelts.

"We will! And we'll see you when we get back!"

They drove off and Jessica went back into the house with Monty.

"This is a bit strange, isn't it boy?" she said. She felt deflated by her parents' reaction to the news of her role. They'd congratulated her, and she knew it was silly to expect more than that from them, but Bethany's mum had insisted upon taking her daughter out for a special dinner with her whole family when she'd heard about her casting, and Bethany was only an understudy.

She was also wondering just what she was going to do by herself while her mum and dad were away. She wasn't used to having a lot of free time — it was usually filled up by ballet-related stuff. Yes, she'd need to train and work out, but with no rehearsals, classes or waitressing work, she'd have hours more available to her every day while she was here.

Her dad had made her solemnly swear that she wouldn't leave Monty alone for more than a few hours at a time because he wasn't used to being left for long periods, so anywhere that she wanted to visit that was further afield than in town itself, she'd have to have him along with her.

She could take him for lots of long walks she guessed. She had use of her dad's car, so maybe she could go hiking for the day? She was still feeling pretty jet-lagged, though, so maybe she'd take it easy today. Of course, taking it easy for Jessica Stone wasn't quite what most people would count as taking it easy.

Jessica had a piece of toast and some peanut butter as that was about all there was left in the cupboards which her mum had carefully emptied before going away, and made a note to pop to the supermarket to pick up some skyr yoghurt and some of her other favourite things to eat. She had a shower and got dressed in leggings and a T-shirt before putting on a touch of make-up and returning downstairs.

The sitting room had the biggest amount of clear space, and Jessica went through her daily exercises as best she could without a barre and a mirror and with a large golden retriever attempting to join in. She struggled to calm her frustration — it wasn't her parents' fault that they didn't have a ballet studio, and it wasn't Monty's fault she was being weird and he didn't understand why. She knew she'd struggle trying to keep fit like this, though. She'd have to figure out a better solution. She had to be in the best shape possible for when rehearsals began. Maybe her rash decision to fly halfway across the world at such a vital point in her career wasn't such a good idea.

Going to the supermarket was something she could do to make things easier for herself and make her feel more in control, so she let Monty out for a wee in the garden, and then grabbed her purse. She considered taking the car but the supermarket was only a few minutes away and it was probably more effort to drive and park than to walk.

It was another lovely day, warmer than yesterday though still mild compared to New York, and Jessica's mood began to lift. She knew she was stuck in her ways. She was very used to only having to think about herself and putting herself first all the time. When she was at home she had the dance studios available to her generally whenever she wanted; it was easy for her to dance in a professional environment within five minutes of her apartment. She couldn't expect to have that here.

The British supermarket was quite a culture shock after so many years of living in the US. There was nowhere near as much choice as she was used to, and she wasn't familiar with any of the packaging anymore. The shopping took her longer than she'd expected, and she hadn't been able to get everything on her list, but at least she had healthy food for the next few days.

Monty was thrilled to see her when she returned, especially when she gave him some of the roast chicken she used to make herself a salad for a rather late lunch.

After she'd eaten, and still tired from travelling the day before, Jessica sat down on the sofa with a coffee and her iPad. She would catch up on some blogs she liked to read by ballet dancers around the world. She wasn't sure of the exact moment she fell asleep, but when she woke up it was five o'clock and Monty was resting his head in her lap and gazing into her face beseechingly.

"I'm so sorry, Monty!" she said. "You must be desperate for a walk!" Getting herself up from the sofa she promptly downed a glass of water and gave her body a stretch to wake herself up. Making sure she had poop bags in her pocket, she attached Monty's lead. She'd decided to head down to the river path by the golf course as her dad had suggested. That would give Monty the opportunity to be off the lead for a bit, and she would quite like to see the area again. She used to love going down there with her dad to get holly and ivy to make a wreath for the front door at Christmas.

Monty was very keen to be on his walk, and her dad hadn't quite been truthful when he said Monty was good on the lead. He pulled Jessica along, forcing her to hold the lead with both hands. She'd have to look up some dog training videos on YouTube because this would drive her crazy if they were going to go on proper long walks together.

They turned into the lane which led down to the golf club. Shortly they'd branch off onto an adjoining footpath which wound down to the river. Fed up with being dragged around, and not seeing any cars about, Jessica let Monty off the lead — it was less than a hundred metres to the gate which signalled the start of the path anyway. Monty sniffed around, sticking close to Jessica, who was ready to grab him at any moment if it looked like a car was coming.

She heard a noise behind her and checked to see if it was a vehicle. It wasn't, but Monty decided to choose that moment to bolt. By the time Jessica turned back around he was already fifty metres away from her and careering round the corner into the golf club car park.

She began to run after him. As she caught up with him in the car park, the reason for Monty's excitement became apparent — he was chasing a squirrel. Jessica made a grab for his collar, but missed, narrowly avoiding losing her balance. She took a second to catch her breath, during which Monty raced off back down the lane again. Cursing the dog, Jessica resumed her pursuit.

She rounded the corner . . . just in time to see Monty run right in front of a black Land Rover. The driver slammed on the brakes. Jessica stopped, horrified and instinctively closed her eyes for a second. On opening them, it was to see Monty excitedly jumping around by the driver's door. She let out a huge sigh of relief. The door opened, and a large man stepped out. A man Jessica had seen before, on her walk the previous day. Only now he looked furious. He slammed the car door shut and, ignoring Monty's exuberant welcome, took hold of his collar and marched him over to Jessica.

"If you can't control your dog, you should keep it on a lead," the man barked. "You're very lucky I didn't run him over, and if I had it would have been completely your own fault."

"I'm so sorry . . ." Jessica began. He was right, of course. Monty was her responsibility. Tears began to well up in the corners of her eyes at the thought of what could very easily have become of Monty. Her dad would have been devastated if the dog had been hurt.

"Make sure it doesn't happen again," the man snapped, not allowing her to explain that Monty wasn't even her dog. He went to go back to his car, but seemed to have second thoughts. He looked at Jessica properly. She thought she saw a hint of recognition there again.

"Do I know you from somewhere?" he asked, his tone softer.

"I wouldn't have thought so," Jessica replied. "I don't live around here. Look . . ."

Her words died away. The man was already back in his car, and she quickly moved to the side of the lane so he could drive past and continue on his way to the golf club car park.

Feeling embarrassed and a bit shaky at the thought of what could have happened, Jessica attached Monty's lead firmly to his collar. "And don't think that's coming off again until you're safely in the house," she told him.

She hung back, wanting to give the man time to get out of his car and out of sight before she continued their walk. She didn't know if he was going to the golf club or down the footpath, but whichever it was, if she let him get ahead, she could stay out of his way while she took Monty for a much shorter walk than she'd originally intended. She had absolutely no desire to bump into that man again.

When she was sure he would be well out of sight, Jessica wrapped Monty's lead around her hand so that he was kept close to her. The dog seemed to understand that he was in an awful lot of trouble and walked much more calmly back round the corner and to the gate leading to the footpath. They got through the gate without mishap and Jessica gave him a little more lead so Monty could have a sniff around. "Good boy," Jessica muttered. Her heart rate had calmed down and she was even beginning to enjoy herself now. Thankfully Monty hadn't been hurt and now that she knew what to expect from him, she would make sure she was much more on her guard.

They wandered along the path for about two hundred metres until it turned and ran alongside the river. The path was cool, shaded by the overhanging oak and sycamore trees. The water looked clear and inviting, sparkling in the late afternoon sun, and if she hadn't had the dog with her, Jessica might have been very tempted to have a swim.

Jessica heard a whistle and a voice calling out, "Dennis, come!" Looking up the path ahead, she saw a springer spaniel who'd been heading towards them, spinning round. A moment later, and the whistler was revealed — the man who'd nearly run Monty over.

Quickly — and because there was nothing for it — Jessica pulled a bemused Monty behind a large tree. She squatted down next to him. "Be quiet," she hissed, urgently. With any luck, the man would just walk right past them.

The man came closer and Jessica held her breath, willing him not to glance in her direction. He walked past and Jessica let out a sigh of relief . . . at the same time as Monty gave a big welcoming woof to his new best friend.

The man looked down towards the noise and immediately spotted Jessica.

"Are you all right?" he asked, his face a picture of bewilderment.

"Yes, thanks," Jessica said as nonchalantly as she could manage in the circumstances. Hopefully he'd carry on his merry way. She'd give him a few minutes to be well out of sight . . . But Monty had other ideas. He was bored of being on the lead. He wanted to play with the man and his dog. He lurched suddenly, pulling the lead out of Jessica's hands.

Thrilled at his new-found freedom, Monty began playing a very energetic game of chase with the springer spaniel.

"Dennis!" the man said crossly, attempting to get hold of his dog, and failing.

Jessica rushed to the dogs, intending to grab Monty by the collar but the golden retriever, misjudging a tight turn, bashed into her legs. Jessica fell backwards and went tumbling down the riverbank, only stopping just before the drop into the water. She screamed as a surge of pain ripped through her. Her foot had landed awkwardly, her full weight upon it.

Panic immediately flooded Jessica's brain — not her foot. Please, not her foot! Monty stood in front of her, staring, his head cocked to one side, his excitement replaced with concern.

Jessica fought to hold back tears, not just at the pain she was feeling, but at the knowledge of what this meant for her

27

career. She'd had enough injuries in her life to suspect this one was going to have her laid up for quite some time.

Very gingerly, she attempted to stand. She let out a squeak as her foot gave way beneath her and promptly sat down again. She was used to pain as a dancer, used to working through it. But her foot really bloody hurt.

She managed to pick up Monty's lead so he wouldn't run off again, though he seemed determined to stay by her side now. She wouldn't be able to walk back to her parents' house, especially with Monty. Could she make it slowly back to the gate and organise a cab to meet her there and take her to the hospital?

"Don't move," the man called from the footpath.

"I'm fine. I just need a minute," Jessica replied through clenched teeth.

"No, you're not," said the man, moving closer to her. "You're hurt. Stay still, I'm coming down to you."

Worried he'd start having a go at her, Jessica explained, "Monty's not my dog. I'm walking him for my dad, who didn't tell me he was so badly behaved. I'm looking after him while my parents are away."

The man made his way to her. "Where does it hurt?" he asked.

"My foot," Jessica said.

"Do you mind if I take a look?" Seeing the unsure look on Jessica's face, he explained, "I'm a doctor."

Jessica nodded her consent and winced as he gently removed her trainer and sock. He carefully examined it, asking her to tell him exactly where the pain was.

"You're going to have to get this checked out. It looks like it's probably a break," he declared.

Jessica's stomach rolled as terror threatened to engulf her. She swallowed hard, forcing her emotions down.

"I will," she managed to mutter.

"Let's get you standing up," the man said, holding out his hand to help her up.

"I'm all right," Jessica insisted. This was embarrassing, and she'd really rather that he left her alone so she could somehow make it back along the path by herself and at her own pace and have the luxury of not having to put on a brave face.

"No, you're not," he replied, firmly. "If you keep hold of your dog's lead, I'll carry you to my car."

"You don't have to do that!"

"You could do more damage if you attempt to walk on it now. If you'd rather do that, I'll gladly leave you alone . . ."

"I don't want to do any more damage," admitted Jessica.

She accepted his offered hand, and once she was on her feet and sure she had Monty firmly by the lead, Jessica found herself swept up into the man's arms. Her foot jarred a little and she bit her lip, not wanting to complain, but the man noticed. "Sorry," he said, his dark brown eyes meeting hers and taking her mind off the pain for an all too brief moment. "I'm being as gentle as I can."

He walked carefully back up the bank, his dog following dutifully behind. Monty looked momentarily confused but seemed happy to go along with this strange new way of going for a walk.

We must make quite a sight, Jessica reflected. Such a strange procession. They rejoined the path, and the man adjusted Jessica in his arms. "Are you comfortable?"

"Yes, thanks. Are you sure I'm not too heavy for you?"

"I'm fine. You're tiny."

He began walking down the path. He smelled of sandalwood and coffee, Jessica noticed, and she found herself closing her eyes and relaxing into his grasp. She must be in shock. How could she be thinking about what some random stranger smelled like at a time like this?

"I'm Nathan, by the way," her rescuer said.

Jessica opened her eyes, embarrassed that she might have been spotted getting so relaxed in his arms.

"I'm Jessica."

"Jessica Stone," Nathan confirmed.

"Yes. How did you know that?"

"We used to go to primary school together. Your mum was one of the teachers. I left the area when my family moved to Somerset in the summer before I was due to start secondary school. I thought I recognised you earlier, but then you said you didn't live around here . . ."

"I don't — I live in New York."

"Wow."

"It's pretty great," Jessica said, mustering a smile. "Wait, I remember you. You used to sit opposite me in Year 6. Nathan Townsend!"

"That's right."

"And you're a doctor now?"

"A GP. I just started at the surgery here about a month ago."

"My mum mentioned something about a new doctor. So, you moved back?"

They'd reached the gate and Jessica was impressed he managed to open it and get both of the dogs through without having to put her down.

"Yes, the job came up, and I remembered being happy here so I applied for it. Dennis, heel," Nathan said, and the dog stuck right by his master as they walked across the car park to Nathan's Land Rover.

Nathan opened the front passenger door and lifted a wincing Jessica into the seat. "Apologies for the dog hair," he said.

He took Monty's lead from Jessica and put the dogs in the back. "I don't have a seat belt for Monty I'm afraid, but if your parents still live in the same house, it's not far."

"You know where my parents live?"

"Yeah." Nathan blushed. "I came to a couple of your birthday parties."

"Of course you did," confirmed Jessica.

"And you had that Halloween party one year."

"Was that the one your little sister was sick at?"

"Yes! I'd forgotten about that!"

30

Nathan started the car and began to drive to Jessica's parents' home. She gritted her teeth when her foot jarred as they went over a speed bump. Jessica had to admit that it was a good thing Nathan had insisted on helping her. She'd probably still be by the side of the river if it wasn't for him. Plus, he'd somehow done an amazing job of distracting from at least some of the emotions threatening to flood her brain and overwhelm her.

Nathan pulled up outside the house. "Thank you," Jessica said. "I really appreciate your help."

"It's not a problem. How will you get to the hospital? Have you got someone you can call to take you as your parents are away? Is there anyone staying with you here?"

"I'm staying by myself," Jessica admitted.

"In that case I'm not leaving you here," he said. "I'm dropping Monty off in the house and then I'm taking you to A & E."

"I can get a cab," argued Jessica. She wished he'd just go and leave her alone.

"The longer you're trying to move around on that foot without it being in a boot or plaster, the more likely you are to do additional damage. It'll be quicker for me to take you and I can help you out of the car at the hospital."

"OK," agreed Jessica reluctantly. He was right: the sooner her foot was seen to, the better. As for Monty, well, she might be hours in the hospital, but there wasn't anything she could do about that. She didn't have the phone numbers for anyone who lived locally who could come and sit with Monty. He would just have to be brave.

"Give me the house keys and I'll put him inside. Do you want anything with you?"

"My handbag from the hallway, please. It's the blue one on the floor. Could you lock Monty in the conservatory? There's a dog bed for him in there."

"No problem."

Nathan hopped out of the Land Rover, and had soon deposited Monty in the house and returned with Jessica's bag.

"Are you absolutely sure you don't mind driving me to the hospital?"

"It's fine. Dennis was partly to blame for you getting hurt in the first place," Nathan said. He fiddled with the radio and settled on a station playing something Jessica recognised by Muse. "Is the music OK?" Nathan asked.

"Yes, thanks."

Things seemed to feel more awkward between them now. Jessica felt stupid for what had happened to her, and bad for taking up Nathan's evening. Most of all, she was terrified of what her injury meant for her career. She was trying to remain positive and hope for the best, but she knew it was impossible that she'd be able to dance when rehearsals began in just a couple of weeks. She'd danced on a sprain before, though. If it was just a sprain, maybe two weeks would allow time for it to heal enough for her to begin rehearsing gently . . . But there was no such thing as gentle rehearsal in a professional ballet company. True, they wouldn't be going all out with their movement for the first weeks of rehearsal, but she'd still be expected to dance for many hours every day. A tear rolled down her cheek as her thoughts ran through her head, and she wiped it away, glancing quickly over at Nathan and hoping he hadn't seen.

They pulled into the hospital car park. "A & E is just to the left," Jessica pointed out. "If you could just drop me by the entrance, I'll be fine from there."

"I'm happy to help you in."

"I can manage," Jessica said, firmly.

"You can't walk."

"I'm sure someone will help me . . ." Jessica looked around as if an obliging medic might just stop beside the car.

Nathan pulled over in the drop-off zone and was by Jessica's door before she had a chance to open it.

"I'm carrying you in at least," he said.

Jessica had to admit there didn't seem any other option. "Thank you," she said into his warm neck as he scooped her up and carried her inside.

They were spotted by a porter who brought over a wheelchair.

"Thank you for everything. I'm sorry for being such a nuisance. You really can go now," she said. The pain was getting worse if anything and she *needed* to be left alone.

"How will you get home?"

"I'll call a taxi."

Nathan shrugged. She felt bad, but told herself not to be silly. She'd thanked him for his help and he'd be grateful to get back to his evening. He was being kind, but she felt vulnerable and scared and didn't want Nathan to see her like this any more than he had already. She was used to looking after herself — and she was good at it. She didn't need his help, although she had to admit she would have been rather stuck without him up to this point. But she'd be fine by herself from here. Principal ballerina Jessica Stone could manage alone and didn't need anyone's pity.

CHAPTER FOUR

Jessica was lucky that it had been a slow night in the Accident and Emergency department so she'd been seen fairly quickly. She considered herself very unlucky however that an X-ray showed one of the middle bones in her foot was broken. The doctor had the foot put in plaster and told her she'd be out of action for at least three months. She was devastated. How could this have happened only two days after she'd been given the opportunity of a lifetime? Jessica was suddenly very, very glad that her mum and dad were both away and she had the house to herself for a week and a half. A week and a half in which she could wallow and work out what on earth she was going to do.

It was just after nine that evening when she was wheeled by a young nurse into the waiting room. "Is there anyone here to pick you up, love?" the nurse asked. "You're welcome to use the wheelchair to get to their car if you like? Remember, it's best that you try to keep your leg elevated as much as you can to help with swelling."

"Thank you. I'll call myself a taxi. I'm happy to wait outside." Jessica was desperate to be out of the light and noise of the hospital.

"All right, if you're sure. Let me at least wheel you out there."

The nurse pushed Jessica through the automatic doors. She handed Jessica a pair of crutches and was about to help her out of the wheelchair when a figure came running over.

"I'll take her from here," said Nathan, stopping beside them.

The nurse threw Jessica a look which clearly conveyed that she approved of her rescuer, and handed the wheelchair containing Jessica over to Nathan.

"There was no need for you to stay." Jessica knew she sounded rude and ungrateful, but she hadn't asked Nathan to hang around. She didn't need him to do some kind of knight in shining armour routine. She barely knew him, he didn't owe her anything, and she didn't want to feel beholden to him. And she couldn't be around anyone right now.

"I know," said Nathan, an edge to his tone. "I was worried about you managing to get home by yourself."

"You think I couldn't manage to catch a taxi by myself?"

"I wasn't sure if a taxi driver would help you in and out of their car. They certainly wouldn't help you into your house, and make sure you've got everything you need before they leave."

He began pushing Jessica's wheelchair across the car park.

"What are you doing?" Jessica hissed. "I said I didn't want your help!"

Nathan stopped, and then pushed the wheelchair to the edge of the car park, away from any oncoming traffic. He put the brakes on and moved in front of Jessica.

"I am more than happy to leave you here," he said bluntly. "I'm hungry, and frankly I had more interesting things to do with my evening than waiting around a hospital car park for you for hours. But I have waited around and I'm here so I may as well drive you home and check that you're all right. Then you never have to see me again. But I will literally be driving past the end of your parents' road to get to my own house."

He stood waiting with his arms crossed for her to respond.

Jessica's first reaction was to insist he push her back to the hospital entrance and leave her alone. But it was dark now. And he did make a good point that he'd be driving right by her parents' house. And he would help her into the house. And her foot really hurt.

"A lift would be lovely, thank you," she said.

"See, that wasn't so hard, was it?" Nathan said. He received a glare in response.

A couple of minutes later, Jessica was comfortably ensconced in the front passenger seat of Nathan's Land Rover, with Dennis attempting to lick her ear from the back seat while she watched Nathan push the wheelchair back into the hospital. He was certainly handsome, she admitted to herself. There was no denying that. But he was also incredibly bossy. And kind, she supposed. She guessed he must be single; a girl-friend or wife wouldn't be too impressed with him spending the evening with some random woman. Or maybe he'd called and explained how pitiful Jessica was lying in the dirt with her broken foot. And how stupid she'd been to let herself get into that situation in the first place.

She was brought back to the present when Nathan opened up the driver's door and climbed into the car.

"You ready?" he asked.

"Yep."

They sat in silence. Jessica was too upset, and still a bit cross with Nathan, to want to talk.

"Would you like some music on?" Nathan asked.

"Only if you do," she responded.

Not long after, Nathan pulled into Jessica's parents' driveway.

Before she could arrange herself and her crutches to climb out of the car, Nathan was round by her door. "Would you like me to carry you in?" he asked, gruffly.

"I think I can manage with the crutches," Jessica found herself saying, although actually she really would have liked to have been lifted up and carried again.

"Can Dennis come into the house?"

"Yes, of course." She didn't even bother arguing that there was no need for Nathan to come in — he'd end up coming in to help her anyway, and she was done with fighting for the day.

Walking with the crutches was an awful lot harder than Jessica remembered from other brief periods when she'd had to use them. Maybe because this injury was more painful than any of the others she'd had and so she was being extra careful with it.

"Why don't you get comfortable on the sofa, and I'll let Monty out of the conservatory. Make sure you keep that foot out of his way," Nathan warned.

Nathan hovered around her as Jessica worked her way through the hallway and into the sitting room. She was very wobbly, so it probably was a good idea that he stayed close by. She could hear Monty whining from the other side of the house. Nathan helped her down onto the sofa and put some cushions behind her, before gently putting some more under her broken foot. Then he went to get Monty, Dennis following in his wake.

A moment later, Monty came running in. "Careful," Nathan warned, and Monty slowed down. "Is he usually fed in the evening?" Nathan asked.

"Oh yes! At six! He must be starving by now!"

"Not to worry, I'll feed him. Where's his food kept?"

"There are some very overly complicated instructions on the fridge," Jessica explained. "Oh, make sure Dennis has some too if he's hungry," she called out after Nathan.

"OK, thanks," he shouted back.

Monty seemed much calmer when he re-emerged after his supper.

"What would you like to eat?" Nathan asked Jessica in a tone which brooked no argument.

"You don't need to . . ." began Jessica.

"I do need to. There is no one else here and you are supposed to be resting and keeping your foot elevated, so you can't cook, and you're going to feel rubbish if you don't eat. Now, is there some pasta or something I can make for you?"

"I don't eat pasta," Jessica said.

37

"Are you coeliac?"

"No."

"What do you eat?" asked Nathan, an edge to his voice. Jessica couldn't blame him. She knew she wasn't being very nice, but she wasn't interested in eating or in having someone to keep her company. She just wanted him to leave so that she could feel sorry for herself.

"Honestly, I'm not hungry. I had a big lunch," Jessica said. She could feel her eyes beginning to fill with tears.

"Are you OK?" Nathan asked, he stepped towards her.

"I'm fine," Jessica reassured him, waving him away, but the tears had already begun to fall.

Nathan crouched down next to her and put his arms around her, bringing her into an unexpected hug which she surprised herself by sinking into. "Are you in a lot of pain?"

"No," Jessica managed to say. "The hospital gave me painkillers, and as long as I keep it still, it's not too bad."

"Then what is it? The thought of me cooking for you can't be that bad." Nathan released her and her body felt the loss immediately.

"It's not that." Jessica accepted the tissue he passed her from the box on the coffee table. Monty put his head on Jessica's good leg, making her flinch.

"Off, Monty," Nathan said gently. He perched on the edge of the sofa. "You don't have to tell me what's upsetting you so much if you don't want to, but it might help if you do."

Jessica took a deep breath. Maybe it would help to speak to Nathan. Someone who didn't know her properly.

"I'm a dancer," she blurted out.

"Oh," said Nathan, realisation flooding his face. "So breaking your foot is really bad news for you."

"You could say that. I'm a ballet dancer and I'm supposed to be starting rehearsals for a new production of *The Sleeping Beauty*. I've been cast as Aurora."

"Wow."

"Yeah, it's my first role as a principal dancer."

"I'm sorry," Nathan said. His kind words set Jessica off crying again.

"This is ridiculous," she said. "I never cry."

"You've had a huge disappointment," Nathan reasoned. "There's nothing wrong with having a bit of a cry about it. It's completely understandable."

"Thanks. I'm trying not to even think about the possibility that there might be permanent damage."

"Take it one step at a time. You did the right thing getting it checked out as soon as possible. You're young and healthy. If you follow the hospital's instructions, it should heal up fine. Did they say how bad a break it was?"

"They thought it looked clean, but the X-ray wasn't very clear. They said that my foot's been under a lot of strain for years, though, with the dancing, which might affect it. They could see there had been a sprain on the same area previously that hadn't healed quite right."

"Have you been in pain with that?"

"Every ballet dancer is in pain with their feet. How can you tell what's regular pain and what's something that hasn't healed properly?"

"I'll have to take your word for it."

"Well, regardless, there's no way I'll be able to start rehearsals."

"No," agreed Nathan. "And if you attempt to dance on that foot too soon, you really will end up with permanent damage. What time is it in New York now? Would someone be at your dance company for you to talk to?"

Jessica checked her watch. "Probably."

"It might be good to rip the Band-Aid and tell them what's happened."

Jessica nodded. This wasn't a telephone call she wanted to make, but it needed to be done. She may as well do it earlier rather than later.

"Could you pass me my phone, it's in my bag?"

"Sure." Nathan handed her the bag. "Why don't I take Monty out for a walk round the block while you're on the

39

phone so he doesn't disturb you? I'll make you a hot drink when I get back. What would you like?"

"A coffee would be great," Jessica admitted, suddenly grateful that Nathan had hung around. "The decaf in the cupboard above the kettle, please."

"No problem, see you in a bit." Nathan left with the dogs.

Jessica steeled herself and dialled the office of her company.

* * *

It took less than ten minutes for Jessica to explain what had happened to the head of the company. She'd been sympathetic, but had dealt with such a number of injured dancers in her career that it had become par for the course.

The good news was that the company's insurance would cover Jessica while she was incapacitated so at least she could still afford her rent and to eat until she was able to work again, as well as medical care for her foot once she was back in the US. The call ended with Jessica promising to keep the company updated, but having formally resigned her part in the *Sleeping Beauty* production.

Jessica heard Nathan and the dogs return as she was finishing the call and was surprised that her reaction was relief at not being alone. Nathan was going to make her a cup of coffee and, right at this moment, that seemed like a really lovely thing.

Nathan stuck his head around the door. "You all done?" he asked.

"Yes, thanks."

"How do you take your coffee?"

"Black, no sugar."

"One sec."

A moment later, Nathan was back with a mug of coffee and a large bowl of food.

"I went to the Chinese and got you some steamed chicken and broccoli," he explained.

"You didn't have to do that!" Jessica exclaimed, though it looked and smelled amazing and her stomach gave a rumble as he handed the bowl over.

Nathan shrugged. "You should eat and I was starving as well and you said you didn't want pasta . . ."

"Sorry. I'm in a really funny mood this evening and I can be fussy about what I eat because of needing to keep in shape for work."

"It's not a problem, I get it." Nathan went back out of the room. He reappeared soon afterwards with his own bowl of food: beef in black bean sauce, and a container of egg fried rice.

He sat on the other sofa opposite Jessica's and Monty and Dennis lay down on the rug in front of the fireplace, keeping a watchful eye out in case either of the humans dropped any food.

"Do you know, I don't think I've ever been allowed to eat in this room before," Jessica said.

"Seriously?"

"Yeah. It was something my mum was really strict about for some reason. We couldn't even have popcorn in here."

"I'm sure she'd allow it this once."

"Maybe," admitted Jessica.

"Do you want some rice with that?"

"Sure, thanks," she said and Nathan brought the rice over and served her. She marvelled at this bizarrely domesticated scene she found herself in with a person she hadn't seen for more than twenty years.

"You chose well for me, thank you," Jessica said in between mouthfuls.

"I just went for the healthiest thing on the menu," admitted Nathan.

"Good strategy."

"So, how long are your parents away for?" Nathan asked.

"They only left today and are booked in for ten nights."

"Will they come back early when they hear what's happened to you?"

"They'll probably want to," Jessica admitted. "But no way am I going to let them. They're away with my brother and his family and they've all been really looking forward to it. Plus my brother's car doesn't have enough space for his family to bring back all of their stuff — my mum and dad had to take some of it in their car, so that would be a complete pain for them."

"How are you going to manage here by yourself, though? Especially with a large dog to look after."

"I haven't finished working that out yet," Jessica said honestly.

"There isn't even a loo on the ground floor here, is there?"

"No, the only bathroom's upstairs."

"You'll have to somehow get up and down the stairs every time you need a pee."

"Yeah . . . I guess I'll go up and down on my bum."

Nathan didn't say anything for a moment and appeared to be thinking.

Finally, he looked up from his bowl and said, "I think you should come back to my house and stay with me."

"What?"

"My study downstairs has a bed in it, and it even has an en suite with a shower. You can bring Monty with you. I'll have to go to work, but at least I can let the dogs out in the morning and at lunchtime, and then walk them when I finish."

"I know you feel bad about my foot, but that's insane. I can't move into your home! And especially not with Monty. I promised Dad I'd look after him — I have no idea what he would do in a different house. He seems like a bit of a loose cannon."

"Monty will be fine. You can keep an eye on him. And you're not moving in, you'd just be staying for a week and a half. I'm guessing you don't really know people around here anymore to help you out, and you won't be safe going up and down those stairs."

The suggestion was so crazy, Jessica honestly didn't know where to begin with all the reasons why it was a really bad idea. "But you don't even know me. I don't even know you!"

42

"I've known you since we were five years old."

"You haven't seen me since we were eleven! You know nothing about me and I know nothing about you!"

"I know that you hate maths and that you have a Furby called Harriet and collect Power Rangers stickers," Nathan joked. "You know that I also collect Power Rangers stickers and like ham sandwiches for lunch."

"Seriously."

"OK, seriously. I don't want you to injure your foot any more than you already have. It's not sensible for you to stay here by yourself, especially not with Monty to look after. I have to walk Dennis anyway, and I always come home at lunchtime to check on him. It's no more work for me to walk Monty — unless he pulls me down a riverbank as well. And my house is a lot better set up for an invalid than your parents' house is."

"That still doesn't change the fact that I don't know you."

"You used to know me and you used to know my family. Plus, as a doctor, I've had criminal record checks so I'm unlikely to be planning to murder you."

"Why would you do this for me though?" Jessica asked. Offering her and Monty use of his home was surely going above and beyond what anyone would generally offer in this situation.

"Because I remember how much you loved to dance. I remember watching you in shows at school — you were brilliant. And the best chance of you being able to get back on that foot as soon as possible is if you have someone to help you."

As crazy as Nathan's plan seemed, there were parts of it that did make sense to Jessica. It would be really hard for her to look after Monty here by herself. But she'd feel she was taking advantage of Nathan if she and her dad's dog took over Nathan's home.

"I'm guessing you live alone, and you don't have a wife or girlfriend you need to check this arrangement with first?"

A shadow clouded Nathan's face. "I live by myself and I'm single," he said quickly.

Jessica wasn't sure he felt very happy about that fact.

"Your idea is completely nuts, but I'll admit it seems like the most sensible thing to do from my point of view. But the deal has to be that you tell me if you want Monty and me to leave. If we get too annoying, or you just want your place back, you have to say so."

"Deal," said Nathan. He came over to Jessica and held out his hand to her — she shook it.

"Right, in that case, let's get your stuff sorted and over to mine. It's getting late and some of us have to work in the morning. Tell me what you need me to pack."

"That's easy. All my stuff is still in my case on the floor of the bedroom next to the bathroom. The only thing I need from the bathroom is my toothbrush. It's the one in the holder on the sink."

"OK, I'll be right back."

Nathan went upstairs and soon returned with Jessica's case. "I'll put this in the car and then come back for Monty's stuff," he said.

Jessica managed to heave herself off the sofa and get upright on her crutches. Nathan was coming back in the front door as she entered the hall. "You all right?" he asked.

"Yeah, it doesn't hurt as much as earlier."

"Let me put the dogs in the car so they're out of your way." He made sure Jessica was safely in the kitchen before calling the dogs and putting their leads on. "Is there a seat belt for Monty in the other car outside? I'm guessing it belongs to your parents."

"Yes, Dad said about it in his notes. The car keys are in the pot by the front door," Jessica said.

"Cool." The dogs obediently followed Nathan out to his Land Rover.

Jessica grabbed her dad's instructions for Monty and started pulling things out of Monty's cupboard that he would need. Was she completely crazy doing this? Would she be

44

better off managing by herself, like she usually did? At least that way she could be as miserable as she wanted and not have to worry about hurting anyone's feelings . . . But she'd promised to look after Monty, and she couldn't do that properly with a broken foot. There was no one else around who could help her, so it looked like the only sensible solution was to accept Nathan's very kind offer.

CHAPTER FIVE

It took Jessica a moment to remember where she was when she woke up the next morning, and to realise there was someone knocking on her bedroom door.

"Come in," she said groggily.

Nathan peeped around the door. "Hey," he said. "I'm heading off to work in a minute. I've let the dogs out and they're in the kitchen. I thought you might like a coffee." He held out a steaming mug.

"Oh, yeah, thanks. That's really kind of you. Come in." Jessica went to sit up and jarred her foot. She winced.

"I also brought you some painkillers," Nathan said, walking across the room and putting the coffee and the tablets on the bedside table. "Did you manage to sleep?"

"Yes, thank you. My foot kept me awake a little, but not as much as I thought it would. The bed's really comfortable."

Jessica tried to tame her hair. Nathan looked completely put together. His hair was damp from the shower and he wore a white shirt and dark grey trousers.

"How's your foot feeling now?"

"Sore," admitted Jessica.

"Hopefully the painkillers will help with that. Is there anything else I can get you before I go? Would you like some breakfast?"

"You don't need to wait on me . . ."

"You're not very good at being looked after, are you?"

"No," admitted Jessica.

"Look," said Nathan. "You're a professional dancer, you know how important it is to eat properly, how vital it is for your body to get energy from food so that it can perform, and most importantly in this case, heal. It's not easy for you to prepare food, so I'm offering to get you some. Nothing fancy. I'm not suggesting I prepare you a full English, but I have Weetabix and I have bread which I am willing to toast for you. Which would you like?"

"Weetabix, please," said Jessica gratefully. Truth be told, she was hungry.

"I'll be right back with your order, milady," Nathan said, bowing as he shuffled backwards out of the room.

He soon returned with Jessica's breakfast.

"Here you go. I'll be off, then. I'll see you at lunchtime. Here's my mobile number in case you have a problem." He handed her a piece of paper with his handwriting on. "I usually have it turned off during clinic, but if there's an emergency, call the surgery. I've put that number on there as well."

"Thank you, Nathan," said Jessica.

"No problem." He gave her a surprisingly shy smile before he left.

* * *

Jessica got up after she'd eaten her cereal. She managed to attempt a shower of sorts with her plastered foot sticking out of the shower door. At least I'm over my jet lag, she thought wryly as she struggled to ease a pair of shorts over her foot. She'd be limited to shorts, dresses and skirts while she was wearing her boot — lucky it was summer. Carrying her dirty bowl and mug out was not going to be easy while using her crutches she realised. She managed the mug, at least, hooked around her little finger.

She hadn't had a chance to look around Nathan's house the night before. She hadn't even seen the outside properly as they'd arrived in the dark. She opened the bedroom door into the hallway. The next door along led to a sitting room, and the kitchen was at the back of the house. The dogs heard her come out and she could hear them moving about excitedly so she went straight in to see them.

She entered the kitchen warily in case one of them bumped her foot, but though the dogs were clearly thrilled to see her, they seemed to understand that she was fragile and wasn't to be jumped around. A large window above the sink looked out over Nathan's garden, which was complete with a potting shed at the end. Jessica opened up the back door to take a closer look, letting the dogs out in front of her.

By the house was a patio with a rusting barbecue and some plastic chairs stacked in a corner; beyond that, a scraggy lawn stretched down to the shed and what looked like an apple tree at the far end. The whole garden was enclosed by a high wooden fence. The sun was already hitting the patio nicely. It was a pretty spot, but seemed a bit neglected and like no one ever really bothered to use it.

She came back inside and heard her phone beep from back in her bedroom. If she wanted to see who was messaging her, she'd have to hobble back in there. She should have thought of that and brought her phone out with her. She could just leave it, but it might be Nathan, and she didn't want him to worry if she didn't answer. She'd have to be more organised if she was to move around as little as possible, at least for the first couple of days of her recovery.

Going back along the hall, she looked up the staircase, but couldn't make out much of what was up there. She wondered what Nathan's room was like.

Even if he hadn't told her, it would have been clear he'd not lived here for long: there weren't a lot of personal items up on the walls, for example, and everything was very clean and new. Like he'd started completely afresh, she guessed.

She made it to her bedroom, followed closely by both dogs, and picked up her phone. The message was from her mum: *Hello, love. We're having a lovely time. Andrew did a barbecue in the garden last night and we're going to Penrith Castle today. Dad's asking how Monty is. Is he behaving himself?*

Jessica sat down on the bed and debated what to reply. She didn't want to lie to her parents, but she knew if she told them what had happened, they'd want to drive straight back to be with her. She was suddenly filled with gratitude for Nathan. Even the last hour had shown how much she would have struggled alone all day with Monty in a house with the only loo upstairs. Nathan might be at work now, but he was able to walk Monty for her and she was certain he'd make sure she was fed tonight. And most importantly, if she needed him, she knew she could call and he would be back within a few minutes. She had absolutely no doubt of that. How funny to trust someone so completely when she knew so little about them.

Monty's fine, and he's made a new friend, she typed. Then she added, *Glad you're having a lovely time! Say hi to everyone from me!*

There. She hadn't lied. She wasn't sure that was the solution for the whole of the rest of her parents' holiday, but it would have to do for now. The dogs looked at her expectantly when she got up. "I can't take you guys for a walk — look," she said, waggling her plastered foot at them. "But I've left the back door open for you so you can go and lie in the sun if you want."

Jessica's foot was aching a lot now. She debated going into the sitting room and getting comfortable on the sofa in there, but she was on the bed already so she shuffled onto it properly, propping up some pillows behind her. She could watch something on her iPad. Or at least she could if she'd remembered to get it out of her suitcase before she'd got comfy. This was frustrating. She really didn't make a good invalid.

* * *

Nathan leaned back into his chair and closed his eyes, pleased to have a few minutes of peace to gather his thoughts. It had been a busy morning in the surgery, but none of his patients had presented anything too taxing, and so he was actually five minutes ahead in his clinic. He'd decided to take a quick break before calling the next patient in.

It was probably a good thing that he hadn't had much time to think that morning, he reflected. If he had he would have to admit to himself just how insane his actions of the previous day had been.

Yes, he felt terribly guilty about Dennis's part in Jessica's accident, but he knew most people would consider he'd more than redeemed himself by taking her to the hospital. No one would expect him to have her as a guest in his house for the next week and a half, especially when they hadn't seen each other for over twenty years.

And the last thing he wanted after what he'd been through was an attractive woman in his home. He'd moved to Bowerbridge for a fresh start. He needed time alone to heal. He'd planned to focus on work, spending his free time with Dennis.

But there had always been something special about Jessica Stone. He'd been smitten from the moment he'd seen her teaching the other girls in their class how to twirl in the school playground. And it seemed nothing much had changed. Except that she was a bit grumpier now. Although that wasn't really fair; anyone would be grumpy in her situation — she was in a lot of pain and had had a major disappointment. He supposed there was a chance she wouldn't be returning to New York, or at least not for quite a while. How patient would her ballet company be with her if her foot took a long time to heal?

Somehow, he suspected Jessica Stone was going to be disrupting his life for a lot longer than just nine more nights.

* * *

Jessica was pleased to hear Nathan's key turn in the lock of the door at ten past one.

She'd left the bedroom door open so the dogs could come and go to the garden, but they'd spent most of their time sleeping by the side of her bed, except when Monty had decided to investigate her loo, causing her to use swear words she hadn't even been aware she knew as she hurried to stop him from helping himself to the water.

Overall, she found their presence quite comforting. They rushed out to the door when they heard Nathan, though, thrilled to have a human return who could move around properly.

"Hey," Nathan said, petting the dogs. "How are you doing?"

"Not too bad. Did you have a good morning?"

"Yeah, busy. Let me make us a bit of lunch. I've only got about forty minutes before I need to get back."

"Thanks. I appreciate you spending your lunchtime checking on me."

"I usually come home to have a play with Dennis anyway," he reassured her.

Jessica followed him along to the kitchen.

"Did the dogs behave for you?" Nathan asked.

"They were as good as gold, even Monty. Mostly."

"Animals can be very perceptive. Maybe they're going easy on you because they know you're hurt."

"If that's the case, then thank you, guys," Jessica said with a laugh.

"Is soup all right for lunch? It's spiced butternut squash." Nathan held up the carton for Jessica to see.

"Sounds yummy."

Nathan put the soup on to warm through.

"If you have a chance before you leave, could you get me a couple of the garden chairs down, please? I thought it would be nice to sit in the garden this afternoon, while the sun's on it."

"Sure, I'll do it now," he said, heading outside. "And then you can get that foot elevated again," he said, sternly.

Jessica smiled. For someone who hated being bossed around as much as she did, she quite liked it when Nathan became all doctory and strict with her. It made her feel looked after.

Jessica followed him outside and watched guiltily as Nathan got chairs down and wiped them clean before drying them ready for her. By the time she'd got herself sat in one with her foot up on another, lunch was ready and Nathan brought the soup out along with some sourdough bread.

"So," he said, sitting down next to Jessica. "If you were home in New York now, what would you be doing?"

"Dancing," said Jessica automatically. "Actually, with the time difference, I'd probably be in the gym right now."

"How many hours of exercise do you do a day?"

"It varies. More when we're rehearsing and performing, but at least six."

"That sounds exhausting!"

Jessica laughed. "It can be, but it's what you have to do if you want to be a ballet dancer. It's what I've done for fifteen years now."

"Since you were sixteen?" said Nathan, quickly doing the maths.

"Yeah. I boarded at a ballet school in London during the week until I was eighteen, and then I auditioned and was offered a place in the ballet company I'm with now."

"That's dedication."

"Yep, but I bet you worked incredibly hard to get through medical school."

"That's true. I think I've blanked most of it out. I survived on about four hours of sleep a night for years, although some of that was so I could fit in some socialising as well," he admitted.

They finished eating and Nathan took their empty bowls into the kitchen and loaded them into the dishwasher. He came back out with a couple of tennis balls. "It's probably a good idea to tire these two out a bit before I head back to work."

Chaos ensued for the next ten minutes as balls flew everywhere. Dennis had been trained to return the ball to the person who threw it and would place it gently in Jessica's lap for her to throw again, which was very helpful, but a bit yucky as it soon got slimy. Monty, however, would race after the ball, invariably missing it and crashing into the garden fence, before running around with it in a circle like a crazy thing and refusing to give it back to Nathan so it could be thrown again.

"You really don't get the point of this game, do you, mate?" said Nathan, gently wrestling the ball off Monty once again.

This was fun, Jessica realised. Completely different to her usual life, the life she had worked so incredibly hard to have, and not at all what she had expected from her trip back home, but fun nonetheless.

* * *

Nathan found he was rushing to finish after his last patient had left at the end of the day. He cleared his desk and packed his bag up quickly, heading out of the doctor's surgery without stopping as he usually did to chat with anyone behind the reception desk. "Maybe he's got a date to get to," said one of the receptionists wistfully to another as they watched the handsome young doctor leave.

The truth was that Nathan wanted to get back to Jessica. He was looking forward to spending the evening with her. It would be nice to have someone to cook for again. He'd have to pop to the supermarket to get some food in . . . he'd take the dogs out first, though.

"Hiya," he called out as he came in through his front door. The dogs came running up to greet him.

"Hi!" came Jessica's reply from the garden. He could tell there was something not right straight away.

He walked quickly through the house and found Jessica in the garden still in the chairs he'd put out at lunchtime. It was clear she'd been crying.

"What's up?" he asked gently, crouching down beside her.

"I had a phone call from my friend, Bethany, this afternoon. She was my understudy for my part in *The Sleeping Beauty*."

"And now she gets to play Aurora?" Nathan finished for her.

"Yeah," said Jessica, blowing her nose. "Usually the part would go to one of the principals as we hadn't even started rehearsing, but as luck would have it, no one is available. They're either injured or committed to other parts. I know she's my friend and I should be happy for her to have this amazing opportunity, but I've worked for so long for that part. It's what I've dreamt of dancing my entire career, and now she's taken it . . . and before you say it, I know she didn't take it, it was given to her . . ."

"It's completely understandable that you'd be upset. It sucks that this happened to you, especially with working so hard."

"Why did it have to be now? Why not years ago when I was in the corps and it wouldn't have mattered so much if I'd had to take a few months off?"

"It's completely unfair, I'm sorry."

"I'm trying to be happy for Bethany," said Jessica, putting her head in her hands.

"I don't think anyone would expect any more from you."

"It was nice of her to call me," said Jessica. "It must have been awkward for her. She's the only one in the company who knew how much I wanted that particular part. Of course, every ballet dancer wants to be a principal, but that part was extra special to me."

"Why's that?" Nathan pulled a chair over for himself and sat down next to her, never removing his attention from her.

"*The Sleeping Beauty* was the first ballet I ever saw. My mum won a couple of tickets to a production in Covent Garden. I was only five at the time and my mum thought I'd

54

be bored, but my dad didn't want to go so she figured she'd brave it with me."

Nathan smiled. "I bet she regretted that when she started having to drive you to classes all the time."

"Oh, yes. She said I was completely mesmerised by the dancing. I cried when it finished because I didn't want to leave the theatre in case the dancers came back out again. The next day my mum found a dance class for me and I never looked back."

"Why don't we see if we can cheer you up this evening?" Nathan suggested. "You've spoken to your company and to your friend, so at least those things are out of the way. I need to take the dogs out, but then we can cook some supper."

Jessica gave him a weak smile. "That sounds nice. Thank you."

"I'll go to the supermarket on my way back. Is there anything you want?"

"Could you get me some plain skyr yoghurt and a bag of frozen berries, please? Do you want the money for them now?" Jessica asked, going to stand up.

"No, we can sort it out later. I'll be back soon, OK?"

"OK." Jessica was so grateful she had Nathan around, not just for the practical stuff he was doing for her, but also so she had someone to talk to.

* * *

While Nathan was out walking the dogs, Jessica took the opportunity to tidy herself up. She hobbled into her bedroom, sat down on the bed, and checked herself in her make-up mirror. For someone who took a lot of pride in her appearance and was frequently judged on it because of her career choice, she thought she looked a fright.

This was the first day for as long as she could remember that she hadn't put her hair up in a chignon for at least part of the time. It would probably do it good to have a break from it, she decided, and gave it a brush, leaving it loose around her shoulders. She put on some concealer and foundation, to hide her puffy eyes as best as she could, and added some eyeliner and mascara. It would make her feel better. Nothing to do with the fact that she'd be spending the evening with Nathan at all. She changed into a clean top. She was feeling excited, she realised. She couldn't recall the last time she'd been excited about spending an evening with a man, unless she was going to be dancing alongside him, of course. It was a nice feeling, and it was certainly good to have her mind taken off her foot, at least a little.

* * *

It seemed like an age until Nathan returned, but when he did he came bearing food and two worn-out dogs.

"I've got some rainbow trout, and I thought we could have some sweet potato wedges and asparagus with it," said Nathan as he unpacked the bags of shopping.

"Sounds yummy. You'll have to let me pay towards food while I'm here, though."

"We'll go halves," said Nathan, easily. "I also got a bottle of this Shiraz I like — will you have a glass with me?"

"I don't usually drink," explained Jessica.

"I've also got some sparkling elderflower if you'd prefer?"

"Actually —" Jessica hesitated — "do you know what? I think I will have a glass of wine. I reckon I deserve it after the afternoon I've had."

"I think so too. This definitely counts as extenuating circumstances." He retrieved two glasses from a cupboard and poured them both a drink before handing one to Jessica. Their fingers brushed as she took it from him, sending a little tingle around her body. A very pleasant tingle, she mused to herself.

"If I get a chair set up for your foot to rest on, you can sit at the kitchen table and be my sous chef," Nathan offered.

"OK, but don't expect too much from me," Jessica warned. "I'm a terrible cook."

"I doubt that." Nathan took out two knives and two chopping boards and placed one of each in front of Jessica.

"No, I really am," Jessica said, laughing. "I think it comes from never really taking the time to learn and never having the patience to wait around for things to cook properly. But then the takeaway food and the delis in New York are so amazing."

"Not quite like in Bowerbridge, eh?"

"No. The food you got last night was lovely," she quickly added, "But there's not a lot of choice."

"I lived in Manchester for about five years before moving here, and there are some amazing restaurants and takeaways there," he said, taking the fish out of its packaging and placing it on his board.

"I bet. How come you moved, was it just for the job?"

Nathan's demeanour shifted, and he was silent for a moment, apparently very absorbed in the trout he was deboning. Eventually, he said, "No, it wasn't just the job. My relationship broke up and I needed a change of scene."

"Oh, I'm sorry to hear that."

"It's fine, but I'd rather not talk about it if you don't mind," Nathan said.

"Of course, not a problem. When did you learn to cook?" Jessica asked to change the subject.

Nathan looked at her gratefully. "I guess I started at university just because it was cheaper than buying prepared food or takeaways, and I found that I quite enjoyed it so I taught myself more."

"And look at you now, gutting fish like a pro! That really does look disgusting by the way . . ."

"It will taste amazing," Nathan promised. "If I scrub the sweet potatoes in a minute, can you cut them into wedges?"

"That I think I can do," said Jessica. Their eyes met and Jessica smiled shyly at Nathan. His eyes travelled down to her mouth and she felt her heart begin to race. Then Monty jumped up at the counter to try to help himself to some fish.

"Monty! Get off!" Nathan said sternly. The moment was lost and the dog was put outside to think about his actions.

* * *

Supper did indeed taste amazing, and the glass of wine Jessica drank relaxed her enough that if it hadn't been for her stupid foot, she would have been having a really good time.

She went to stand so she could help to clear the table. "Don't you dare," said Nathan immediately. "You know what the doctor said, you still need to be staying off it as much as possible for the first forty-eight hours."

"I feel bad letting you do all the washing-up."

"Well don't. It's fine. Most of it gets chucked in the dishwasher anyway. It'll only take a few minutes."

He opened the back door to let the dogs out into the garden — Monty having been permitted re-entry after a further talking-to.

"You can amuse me with tales from the ballet world while I scrub away at the fish pan."

Jessica laughed. Nathan was so easy to be with and to talk to. She loved how she could relax with him, not having to keep up the facade she usually maintained. Most of the people she knew were in the business of ballet, and if she showed any weakness they would use it against her, or at least they had the potential to. Not that they were all bad people by any means, but they were working towards the same goal as she was, and they were very aware that they might not reach it. She could hardly complain; she was exactly the same.

"So there was one time in Paris . . ." she began.

* * *

They finished clearing up and Nathan made coffees which they drank while they chatted together at the table. He'd just finished telling Jessica about how he'd got Dennis from a dog rescue, when Jessica found herself thinking how handsome he looked. Maybe it was because he'd cooked for her and was looking after her so well . . . and they'd had that moment earlier, she mused.

"I had something that I'd planned to do last night, that I'd kind of like to do now," Nathan said once the clearing up was all done. "But I'm worried you'll tease me."

Jessica's cheeks flushed. Oh, for heaven's sake, she told herself sharply — get a grip. He's not talking about anything with you. Most of the time he's spent with you recently was when you were either crying or covered in mud.

"What is it?" she managed to croak.

"Promise you won't tease me?"

"I can't promise that!" Jessica exclaimed. "It's my moral duty as your friend to tease you if you're doing something embarrassing."

"We're friends, then?"

"Of course we are. I'd feel really bad about taking over someone's home and having them wait on me hand and foot if they weren't even my friend," Jessica quipped. She could feel her cheeks heating up again. "Anyway, stop changing the subject. What did you want to do?"

"Come through to the sitting room and I'll show you," Nathan said, before adding, "Carefully."

Jessica had poked her head into the sitting room but hadn't been in there properly before. It was nice — very clean and tidy like the rest of the house, and without much of anything personal in it.

There was a large cardboard box in the corner. Nathan helped Jessica get settled on the sofa and put cushions underneath her foot so it was elevated. When he was quite sure she was comfortable, he went over to the box and opened it up. The dogs sniffed the box, but decided it wasn't anything interesting and both climbed up to sleep on the second sofa.

"I didn't take you for someone who'd let his dog lie on the sofa." Jessica laughed at how comfortable the dogs had made themselves.

"It's his house as well." Nathan shrugged.

"Fair enough."

"Though in honesty, that was one of those pick your battles things. I was determined not to allow him on there, but he was more determined to be on there, so I gave in on that one."

"I don't think I could bring myself to chuck him off when he looks so cosy."

"Exactly," Nathan agreed. "So, do you like playing computer games?" he continued, pulling some leads out of the box.

"I honestly don't think I've ever played a video game in my life," Jessica said.

"Seriously? How is that possible?"

"I don't know. I guess I just never had the time to."

"Well, now you do."

"My brother, Andrew, had a PlayStation, but I wasn't allowed to touch it."

"Can't say I blame him. I wouldn't have let my sister touch this if my mum and dad hadn't made me." Nathan produced a games console from the bottom of the box. "I present to you my Xbox 360. I was given this bad boy for Christmas when I was fifteen. I was the envy of all my friends for months."

"I bet."

"My mum dropped it off when she came to visit a couple of weeks ago. She didn't want it cluttering up her house anymore."

"I can't understand why . . ." Jessica said with a giggle.

Nathan shot her a look. "You can make yourself useful by untangling these cables. I'm going to check that the TV has the right sockets."

"I think I've drawn the short straw here — these are as bad as Christmas lights."

"Stop complaining and get untangling, or I won't make you a cup of coffee in a minute."

"Yes, sir!"

The wires weren't as badly knotted as Jessica had thought, and it only took a few minutes for Nathan to set up the machine. He handed Jessica one of the controllers. "What do you want to play?" he asked.

"Honestly?" said Jessica. "I have no idea about computer games."

"Well, they're much more fun to play with someone else, so please play one with me. Just for half an hour?"

"OK," said Jessica with an exaggerated sigh. "Half an hour, and only because you cooked me such a nice dinner."

"Hooray! What sort of game would you like? The football ones are pretty simple to pick up."

Jessica screwed up her nose in disdain.

"Fair enough . . ." muttered Nathan.

"What's your favourite?" Jessica asked.

"*Fable II*," Nathan said immediately. "I bought a second-hand copy after I finished my A Levels. I spent days of that summer holiday playing it. It's a wonder I managed to pull myself away from it for long enough to go to university."

"What's it about?" asked Jessica suspiciously.

"It's like an adventure game. You're the hero and there's the main quest and then loads of little quests you can do. It's fun, I promise."

"OK, I believe you. Definitely sounds better than a football game anyway."

"Right, I'll be the main player, and you be the secondary player so you'll need to stay near me, but it means I can show you around."

"Man, you even get to boss me around in the video game?"

"Yep, 'fraid so."

"Half an hour, right?"

"I swear."

* * *

"It's 1 a.m., Jess. I've got to go to bed — I've got work in the morning," Nathan said, rubbing his eyes.

"I know, I know, I'm sorry! I just want to explore that creepy old mansion on the hill for some treasure, and then I promise we can stop. And since when did you call me Jess?"

"Since you took over as main player because I'm apparently not 'forceful enough during confrontations with gargoyles'. I won't call you Jess if you'd rather I didn't. It just seemed like a natural thing to call you."

"It's fine," she said. Somehow his calling her by the shortened version of her name served to make them seem closer, like real friends. She liked it.

* * *

Nathan didn't look quite as put together when he brought Jessica in her cup of coffee the following morning. He was obviously someone who needed his eight hours of sleep every night.

"Don't expect this kind of treatment every morning," he warned. "This is only while you're supposed to be keeping your weight off your foot."

"Thank you," said Jessica. "And I'm sorry I kept you up so late last night."

"It's my fault for introducing you to the game, though I did warn you it was addictive."

"That Lord Lucien has got to pay for his behaviour! He can't be allowed to get away with it!"

"He won't," said Nathan laughing. "I'm guessing you'd like to play some more this evening?"

"Yes, you'll have to cook by yourself I'm afraid because I'm going to need to do a lot of blacksmithing to be able to afford the sword I'm after. And then I think we need to go hunting for a wife."

"I'm beginning to regret this . . ."

"Nothing you can do about it now," said Jessica with a grin and a shrug.

CHAPTER SIX

The day went by slowly for Jessica while Nathan was at work. She really did make a terrible invalid, mainly because she wasn't used to having time to fill. She needed a project to keep her busy — but what? The video game was really fun, but most of what made it fun was playing it with Nathan; it wouldn't be nearly as good doing it by herself.

As the day was overcast and cooler, Nathan took the dogs out for their walk when he came home at lunchtime so they'd have more time for *Fable II* in the evening. Jessica only saw him for a total of about ten minutes when he made them both a tuna and bean salad and bolted it down before he needed to get back to the surgery.

She wished there was something nice she could do for him, but it was tricky without being able to move around much, and she knew Nathan would be cross if she overdid it. Though not as cross as she'd be with herself. As frustrating as it was to be so restricted in what she could do, she knew it was really for the best that she follow doctor's orders to the letter and give herself the best chance of her foot healing up quickly and well. She couldn't allow herself to contemplate what she'd do if her foot didn't mend properly and didn't regain its previous strength.

Nathan was home soon after his clinic ended. Jessica wondered if he'd hurried back to be with her, or if he usually left work so promptly.

"I'll stick some baked potatoes in the oven," Nathan said, "and we can get started."

"Great. I'm the primary player, though," said Jessica. "I've basically spent today working out what we need to do, and it would take me too long to explain it all to you."

Nathan laughed. "Are you always this competitive?"

"Yes," admitted Jessica. "You've got to be really competitive to make it as a ballet dancer, especially if you're a woman."

Nathan raised an eyebrow.

"There are fewer male ballet dancers," Jessica explained, "So it's less competitive. Though I guess it's still more competitive than most careers."

Jessica's mobile rang. She looked at the caller ID and her face fell.

"Is it your friend again? The one who's been given your role?"

"No, it's Mum. I don't know what to say to her because I haven't told her about my foot yet." Seeing the surprise on Nathan's face she said, "I didn't want her to worry. She'll want to come back and that would ruin everyone's holiday."

Her phone stopped ringing.

"I think you should tell her," he said. "You can reassure her that you're fine, but she'll be upset when she gets back if she finds out you've lied to her."

"You're right. She will be hurt if I keep it from her, even if I am being looked after fairly well." Jessica smiled. "I'll call her back."

"Let me help you get comfortable on the sofa."

"Don't worry, I'm all right," said Jessica. It was lovely how Nathan fussed over her.

She got settled on the sofa, and taking a deep breath, dialled her mum on a WhatsApp video call.

"Hi, Mum," Jessica said when Sarah answered. "Sorry, I missed your call."

"Don't worry, darling. Thanks for phoning back. Where are you?" Her mother squinted at her phone.

"Funny story," said Jessica. "Do you remember Nathan Townsend? He was in my year at primary school."

"Of course. He's the new doctor I told you about. Lovely boy. He was so sweet on you."

"Was he?" Jessica asked, a grin spreading across her face. "Anyway," she said, realising she needed to keep on topic, "I'm in his house."

"Oh," said her mum, sounding surprised. "I haven't had a chance to chat with him yet, but I've seen him walking his dog."

"That's right, Dennis."

"And you've gone round to his house to say hello, have you?"

"Not exactly, Mum. I'm actually staying here while you're away," Jessica explained. "With Monty," she added quickly.

"You're staying with him," Sarah repeated.

"Yes. I fell over the other day. I didn't tell you because I didn't want you to worry. Anyway, I broke my foot." Jessica decided not to add Monty's part in it.

"Oh no!" said Sarah immediately. "How badly?"

"It looks like a clean break from what they could tell on the X-ray, but I've got a cast that I need to wear for six weeks."

"And then after that?"

"A lot of rehabilitation. I won't be able to dance for at least three months."

"So, what's going to happen about *The Sleeping Beauty*?"

"My part's been given to my understudy." Jessica was proud of herself for managing to hold back her tears.

"Oh, darling, I'm so sorry. What a disappointment. Are you OK? What are you going to do for money?"

"The company's insured if something like this happens, so I'll be OK for money."

"That's something, at least. Oh, you poor thing," said Sarah. "But . . . that still doesn't explain why you're staying at Nathan's house."

"Nathan was there when I fell and he took me to A & E. He was worried about how I'd manage by myself with Monty and with the only bathroom upstairs in your house and so he offered to have me stay here. He's been really kind."

"Thank goodness for Nathan. He's right, you wouldn't have been able to manage our house. I can't believe you didn't tell me before! I would have come straight home."

"I know you would, and that's exactly why I didn't tell you. I didn't want to spoil your holiday. I'm fine. I'm more than fine — Nathan's taking really good care of me."

"Are you sure? I can take the train back and Dad can stay here . . ."

"Honestly, Mum. I'm sorry I didn't tell you before, but Nathan's taking really good care of Monty and me. It'll be lovely to see you when you get back, but please don't cut your holiday short for me."

"All right, but if you change your mind, just let me know and I can be home in a few hours. It's so good of Nathan to step up and help you. He was always such a kind boy."

"He's been brilliant. Anyway, are you having a good time?"

"Lovely. The children have been in the swimming pool for hours every day, and we've had some wonderful walks. I'll send you some photos once we've finished talking."

"Great. I'd better go now. I need to give Nathan a hand making dinner."

Sarah chuckled. "I never thought I'd see my girl so domesticated! Nathan's obviously having a good effect on you. I'll speak to you soon. And remember, if you need me, I'll be home right away."

"Thanks, Mum."

The call ended and Jessica had to admit that Nathan had been right: she did feel much better now that she'd told her mum the truth.

Nathan popped his head around the door. "Just checking you'd finished. How did it go?"

"Really well — thank you."

"Not a problem. Can we finally get started on some *Fable II* now, please?"

"Absolutely!" Jessica said with a huge smile.

"Also, it's Saturday tomorrow, so I don't need to get to work."

"You shouldn't have reminded me of that. Now there's no chance of you getting to bed at anything like a civilised hour."

* * *

Jessica woke up the next morning and smiled. The previous night had been so much fun. She couldn't believe that such a terrible thing had happened to her career, the kind of thing she'd always dreaded happening and she'd heard horror stories about, and yet she was waking up with a smile on her face having spent another lovely evening with Nathan. It wasn't that he had ignored her injury or the magnitude of what it meant for her career, but he'd instead helped her to focus on other things and not become overwhelmed by her broken foot. She was doing the best she could to help it heal as quickly as possible, and that was all she could do.

And now it was the weekend and he didn't need to go to work for the next couple of days. Yikes, Jessica suddenly thought to herself. They were going to be together for the next two days. What would they find to do and talk about? They couldn't play video games the whole time, surely. Maybe he'd already made some plans that didn't involve her. That would be completely understandable. It's not like he was obliged to hang out with her for the entire weekend. He must have friends. He could even have a date. That's what regular single people who weren't obsessed with their careers did on a Saturday night, wasn't it — go out on a fun date? She'd only been staying with him for a few days so it was completely probable that he'd made plans for the weekend before knowing he was going to end up having her stay.

Well, if he did already have stuff planned, she'd just have to entertain herself. She was a grown-up, after all . . .

Goodness, it was frustrating not being able to exercise. For someone used to spending a vast portion of her day pushing her body to its limits, sitting around with nothing to do didn't come naturally.

She heard Nathan moving around upstairs, opening up curtains and then what sounded like opening drawers. His footsteps came down the stairs and he was greeted enthusiastically by the dogs before going into the kitchen.

A few minutes later, Jessica heard the now familiar knock on her bedroom door and she called out, "Come in!"

"Good morning," Nathan said cheerfully. "I come bearing coffee and happy tidings."

"Are you always so chirpy on the weekend?"

"Unfortunately, yes. Do you want to hear my happy tidings?"

"Go on, then. Thank you for the coffee."

"It is now well over forty-eight hours since you had your accident, so you are officially allowed to move around more!"

"Hooray," said Jessica, sarcastically. "I get to be fractionally more mobile on crutches!"

"And, you don't have to keep your foot elevated all the time, although you still should as much as possible."

"The excitement's too much!"

Nathan threw her a mock glare. "I guess you don't want to hear about what I thought we could do this weekend, then . . ."

"You don't have to spend your whole weekend with me . . ."

"Have you got better things to do this weekend?" teased Nathan. "Do you have a whole gang of friends around here that I don't know about?"

"No," admitted Jessica.

"Neither do I, so we may as well spend the time together. As painful as it appears that would be."

"It wouldn't be painful at all," said Jessica, quickly. "Unless I tried to run on my bad foot. I just don't want you to feel obliged to spend the whole weekend with me if you've other stuff you'd rather do."

"I really don't," said Nathan. "Because I only moved back here recently, the only people I know are from the surgery. It'll be nice to have someone to hang out with."

"All right, if you're sure . . ."

"I'm sure. I'm going to go for a run now."

"Show-off," muttered Jessica.

Nathan ignored her and continued, "But then why don't I think of somewhere we can go for a few hours?"

"Where have you got in mind?" asked Jessica.

"Why are you always so suspicious?"

"It's in my nature."

"Just be ready to go when I get back. I'll take Dennis with me."

"You don't fancy attempting a run with Monty?"

"Nope." Nathan laughed. "See you in a bit."

* * *

Jessica got up and showered, watched by Monty, and drank her coffee as she dressed and put on some make-up. She couldn't help feeling a bit excited about what Nathan had planned for them. She knew she still shouldn't walk much so options would be limited, but it would be nice to go out and do something different.

She wore a dress, feeling the desire to make a bit of an effort as she'd spent the last few days living in shorts and T-shirts, and decided to put her hair up in a loose bun so it was out of her way. When she gave herself a once-over in the mirror, she was surprised to see how relaxed she looked. Her eyes were bright, and the rest and sleep of the past few days meant her skin looked healthier than it had in years.

She used her crutches to go through to the kitchen and make herself some breakfast. She really would have to watch that she didn't overdo it now that she was allowed to walk around more. She'd definitely need to start exercising again though. She'd look up some exercises she could do either sitting or lying down.

It still seemed strange to be in Nathan's house, especially when he wasn't there. She felt bad about nosing about in his home when she was looking for things in his kitchen, and she was very careful to tidy up after herself — he seemed to be a far neater person than she was, and she didn't want him to resent her being there because of the mess she caused.

She was rinsing out her bowl when Nathan and Dennis returned from their run. Dennis had obviously had a lovely time and came straight over to say hello to Jessica, who scratched his ears for him. She had to admit he was a cute dog. However, it was his owner who properly took up her attention. Now he was wearing very well-fitting running shorts and a top, Jessica could make out more of his body than she'd been able to previously, and she found herself analysing him — in the same way she did the bodies of the men she danced with, she told herself. He was quite tanned for someone who spent their weekdays working inside, and his arms and legs were muscular . . . gym sessions, maybe? Though she imagined he was more of a kickabout in the park kind of guy. He was bulkier than the male dancers she knew, which she kind of liked, and she couldn't help remembering how he'd carried her along the path to his car. Obviously, she was used to men lifting her while she was dancing, but Nathan's hold had seemed more protective and caring, as he'd done his best to ensure he didn't bump her foot and jolt her unnecessarily.

"How was your run?" she managed to croak.

"Good, thanks. I'll just have a quick shower to freshen up and then we can get going. Don't forget to put on sunscreen."

"With skin like mine, I never forget," replied Jessica. "Are you going to tell me where we're going?" she asked, watching him jog up the stairs.

"Nope." He disappeared round the top of the staircase.

* * *

Twenty minutes later, the dogs and a rucksack with water bottles and snacks were in the car and they were ready to go.

"You look nice," said Nathan, looking Jessica up and down and making her blush.

"Am I overdressed?"

"No, you just look nice," he replied simply.

"Are you really not going to tell me where we're going?"

"No, but don't get too excited — I'm not going to let you overdo the walking only a few days after you've broken your foot. I thought it would just be nice for you to have a change of scene for a while."

"Can I at least know how long it's going to take to get there?"

"I suppose that's fair." Nathan smiled. "It's only about twenty minutes in the car. I didn't want you to be too long without being able to elevate your leg if you need to."

"Thank you," Jessica said. "And thank you for taking me out, wherever we end up."

"It's my pleasure."

Nathan drove out of the town and into the countryside. The day was overcast but warm. They drove in companionable silence, with Radio 2 in the background.

The roads were all familiar to Jessica and memories of being driven along them to various ballet competitions, shows and rehearsals came flooding back. How her mum and dad must have wished for a weekend off from driving around sometimes, she thought.

They turned off the main road onto a private lane and Nathan drove along it until they rounded a corner and found a grand medieval manor house laid out in front of them, looming over an ornate walled garden.

"Bowerbridge Manor! I remember this!" Jessica said immediately. "We came here with the school."

"I wondered if you'd remember," Nathan said with a grin. "I haven't been since we came on that trip. Matthew Brown fell in the pond over there. I thought it would be a nice place to bring the dogs, and there are plenty of benches for you to take a break on."

"This was a really good idea," said Jessica. It was a perfect day to be outside. "I'd forgotten all about poor Matthew! He had to travel home on the coach still soaking wet, didn't he?"

"Yes, I was sitting next to him and he stank of pondweed."

"That is unfortunate," said Jessica, laughing.

"There's a café here which is supposed to be good, so why don't we have a little wander and then we can grab a coffee and you can give your foot a rest?"

"Sounds good."

The gardens were lovely. The manor house was also open to visitors, and they'd gone in on their school visit, but they couldn't with the dogs and Jessica's foot definitely wouldn't be up to walking around the house anyway. Plus, it was too nice a day to be inside.

Jessica was getting more comfortable on her crutches, though was still wary of the dogs banging her foot by mistake as they ran around her. Nathan kept Monty on the lead as he couldn't be trusted like Dennis could to come back when called.

Visiting somewhere like this definitely wasn't something Jessica usually did, but it turned out to be a very good idea of Nathan's. The pathways were flat enough for Jessica to navigate, and the multitude of available benches meant she was never far from one if she needed to take a break.

The air was filled with floral fragrances and the sounds of the stream which ran through the grounds.

With it being the weekend, there were quite a few people around, mainly couples, though there were also some families. Jessica and Nathan took a side path which led through a gate into a deserted meadow.

"We could let Monty off his lead here so he can have a run about with the ball," Nathan said, looking around for possible doggy escape routes. "It looks enclosed."

"Sure," agreed Jessica.

"And there's a bench there under those trees for you to rest on," Nathan pointed out.

They walked over to the bench and Jessica sat down. Nathan let Monty off the lead, and the two dogs immediately started chasing each other.

"I guess they don't need a ball then," Nathan said, sitting down next to her. "How's your foot feeling?" he asked.

"Achey," Jessica said honestly.

"Let's get it elevated. Pop your legs up on me."

Jessica gingerly eased her legs up so they rested on Nathan's lap. She was very aware that she was wearing a dress and was glad she'd rather precariously shaved her legs in the shower earlier.

"Relax," Nathan said gently. "I won't bite."

Jessica did her best to relax her muscles, but it wasn't easy being so close to Nathan. Was she sweaty? Why was she feeling so awkward? She was a dancer — her work meant she was used to being close to men, much closer than this, and wearing far less, to be honest.

Nathan fiddled in the rucksack next to him and retrieved a bottle of water. "Would you like some?"

"Sure," Jessica replied. It appeared she could only speak in monosyllables when she was this close to Nathan.

"Are you all right?"

"Yes," Jessica squeaked. She cleared her throat. "I'm fine. It's lovely here." It's especially lovely in this position, she thought to herself.

"I'm appreciating it much more now than I did when I was nine," Nathan said. "Shall we give the dogs and your foot a few more minutes and then head to the café?"

"That sounds great. I could murder a coffee."

"I think I remember coming to this part to let off some steam before getting on the coach to go back to school."

"I recall being very put out that there wasn't a playground here," admitted Jessica.

"I still am." He put his hands behind his head and leaned back against the bench.

When the dogs had finished chasing one another, and Monty looked like he was considering causing some trouble,

Nathan got up to throw some balls. Jessica immediately missed his presence.

"Do you think your leg's up to walking to the café now?" Nathan asked.

"Yeah." Jessica accepted Nathan's steadying hand as she got up and sorted her crutches out. "It's feeling quite a bit better now."

Nathan put Monty on his lead, and the quartet went back through the gate and into the house grounds proper, making their way to the east wing of the stately home, where the coffee shop was sited.

"It's just about lunchtime, and I'm starving," said Jessica. "Can I buy you lunch? As a little thank you."

"That would be lovely, but there's no need to at all."

"Are you OK ordering and I'll stay outside with the dogs?"

"Sure. What do you want?"

Jessica deliberated; there wasn't much dancer-friendly food on the menu, but she wasn't going to be training for a while so she could relax with what she ate — at least a little — and she knew what she really fancied.

"Um . . . a black Americano and a cheese and ham toastie, please. Here, take my purse."

Nathan returned with drinks a couple of minutes later. Dennis had curled up under the table and gone to sleep, but Monty was not being nearly as obliging. He was getting himself and his lead nicely wound around a table leg.

"Why don't I take him for you?" offered Nathan. "He's liable to have your chair over."

"I need to be able to control him . . ." Jessica leaned down and unravelled the lead as best she could.

"Sure, but I don't want him to pull you over and hurt you. I've been working on him a bit when I've been out with him, but I haven't had a chance to take him to a café or restaurant before."

"Thank you," Jessica said, gratefully handing the lead over to him. "I noticed that he was walking better on the lead today, but I thought it must just be chance."

"He's coming along really well."

"Training my dad's dog for me really is going above and beyond the call of duty, you know."

"I'm walking him at the moment so it's kind of in my own interests to help him. He's a good boy." Nathan scratched Monty on his head. "Come here, Monty," he said and steered Monty over to sit next to him so he was out of the way.

A waitress came over with their food. Dennis knew better than to beg, but Monty's nose appeared on the table, his eyes beseeching Jessica for a corner of her sandwich. Spotting her wavering, Nathan said, "If you give him some, he'll be driving you mad for the rest of your meal."

"I know, but he looks hungry."

"You know he's not really that hungry." Nathan laughed. "Why don't you keep him a bit for when you're finished?"

Jessica kept a corner for Monty and one for Dennis, and when she and Nathan were finished eating and ready to leave, she stood up, got the dogs to sit, and gave them each their corner.

"Do you want to walk around some more, or are you done?" Nathan asked.

"I'm afraid I think I'm done," admitted Jessica. Her foot was definitely aching a lot more than earlier even with the two lots of sitting. She checked her watch. "Hooray, I can take my next lot of painkillers."

Nathan looked worried. "I hope you haven't overdone it."

"I'm sure I haven't. I'm sorry. It would have been nice to have stayed here for longer."

"Don't worry. Let's get you home," said Nathan cheerfully.

"Can we play *Fable II*?"

"Of course we can," Nathan replied with a smile she suspected was humouring her.

They walked slowly back to the car park. Nathan got the dogs into the back of the Land Rover and then helped Jessica.

"Thank you for bringing me here," she said.

"It was my pleasure."

"And thank you so much for looking after me so well."

"That has also been my pleasure."

"I really doubt that."

"It has," Nathan replied firmly.

"You've really been enjoying spending all your free time with a bad-tempered ballerina who can't even care for her father's out-of-control dog?"

"Monty isn't out of control," he said kindly. "He just needs a bit more training. And you're much less bad-tempered since I introduced you to video games."

Jessica smiled.

"Seriously though," Nathan said, "I'm glad I've been able to help. It's . . . been nice to have someone else around the house. I think I've been getting a bit fed up with my own company."

"It's been nice staying with you," Jessica said. "And not just because I need your help. I think I would have been really lonely staying by myself at my mum and dad's."

"It sounds like it's worked out well for the both of us, then."

CHAPTER SEVEN

"How can you be a doctor and eat that rubbish?" asked Jessica incredulously the following morning, gesturing at the packet of Coco Pops Nathan was pouring himself a large serving from.

"It's my Sunday morning treat." He added milk to his cereal. "And it's fortified with vitamins and minerals. It says so on the box."

Jessica shook her head in mock exasperation. She sat at the kitchen table wearing her pyjamas and eating a bowl of skyr yoghurt with honey and raspberries. The radio was chattering away in the background and the back door was open, allowing in a gentle breeze. The dogs were already sunning themselves on the patio.

Jessica was loading her bowl into the dishwasher when the doorbell rang. Both dogs ran out into the hall barking crazily.

Nathan looked at Jessica and shrugged — he seemed to have no idea who might be visiting on a Sunday morning either. He went to see who it was. Jessica frowned, realising she resented this intrusion into her time with Nathan. She'd been enjoying just being the two of them.

"I tried to call yesterday, but you didn't answer, and then I attempted again this morning," said a female voice.

"Sorry, Mum. My mobile must be out of battery."

"I was passing close by, and I had a couple more boxes of your childhood stuff to drop off. I hope it's OK for me to pop in." The woman's voice rose as she spotted Monty, "Who are you then? Did you get another dog?"

Before Jessica could think of somewhere to hide her pyjama-clad self, Nathan's mum appeared in the kitchen doorway. "Oh, hello," she said. "I'm sorry, Nathan, I didn't realise you had company. You should have said." His mother didn't look best pleased with what she saw.

"You didn't give me much of a chance," muttered Nathan. "This is Jessica, Mum, Jessica Stone. We went to primary school together."

"Jessica Stone? My daughter was sick at your birthday party, wasn't she?"

"She certainly was," said Jessica, shaking Nathan's mum's hand.

"How are your parents? What do you do now?"

"My parents are good, thank you. They're away on holiday at the moment with my brother and his family. I'm usually a ballet dancer. I dance with a company in New York, but I'm a bit laid up at the moment." She lifted up her plastered foot to illustrate her point.

"That is unfortunate."

"Your son has very kindly been taking care of me and Monty while my parents are away. I broke my foot the first day they were gone," Jessica explained. As the realisation dawned on Nathan's mum that Jessica and Nathan weren't an item, she seemed to relax a little.

"Would you like to stay for a cup of tea, Mum?"

"If you're sure I'm not disturbing anything," she said, looking at them both in turn.

"You're honestly not," said Jessica, quickly. "In fact, if you'll excuse me, I'm going to have a shower and get dressed."

"Of course. It was lovely to see you again, Jessica."

"You too, Mrs Townsend."

"Oh, call me Annie, please."

Jessica scurried to her room as quickly as she could with a broken foot. That was embarrassing. Nathan's mum had clearly thought there was something going on between Jessica and Nathan, and for whatever reason, she hadn't been happy about it. Though what business it was of his mother's who her 32-year-old son chose to date, Jessica didn't know. And why wouldn't his mother approve of Jessica? She was a catch! Any mother should be thrilled if her son was lucky enough to date her!

She guessed she could at least see where his mother's confusion lay: the whole scene had looked pretty cosy. But as handsome as Nathan was, the last thing Jessica needed was to complicate her life with thoughts of romance. She was going to be back to New York soon. Though how she was going to manage going up and down the stairs to her apartment, she had no idea.

She took her time showering and getting dressed so that Nathan could have some time with his mum. She was done and preparing to go and be sociable again when she heard them coming back down the hallway and opening the front door.

"Does Claire know about your house guest?" Jessica heard Annie ask.

Who on earth was Claire? Jessica pressed her ear against the bedroom door to better hear the reply, but the pair had gone out of the house, and she couldn't make out anything. She went over to the window, which looked out onto the street at the front of the house, and peeked around the edge of the blinds. Nathan and his mum were chatting by what was presumably her car. After a minute, Annie opened the boot and Nathan lifted out a large cardboard box. Jessica moved away from the window as he began walking towards the house.

It would look strange if she didn't come out to say goodbye, so she forced herself to come out of her bedroom. Nathan was heading back in with a second box and smiled at her as he passed. His mum was closing up the boot of her car.

"Goodbye, Annie," Jessica called out and received a stiff wave in return. It seemed Nathan's mother wasn't completely convinced of the platonic nature of her and Nathan's relationship.

* * *

Nathan was back a couple of minutes later.

"Sorry about that," he said. "One of the perils of having your mother live only a twenty-minute drive away."

"Don't be daft," Jessica replied. "It's your house — you should be able to have anyone you want to visit. It's nothing to do with me. I just wish I hadn't been in my pyjamas, but that was my fault."

"You feel free to be in your pyjamas as much as you like. I'm quite fond of them."

Was Nathan flirting with her? Jessica smiled awkwardly.

"Would you like to take the dogs out for a walk with me again today? We could drive somewhere nice."

"Would you mind if I bowed out? My foot's still hurting from yesterday," Jessica said. Her foot was possibly aching a tiny bit more since yesterday's walk, but only an hour ago she would have jumped at the chance of going out with Nathan again. Now she felt she needed some time to think.

"Not at all. You rest your foot, and I'll be back in a couple of hours."

"OK, thank you."

Jessica breathed a little sigh of relief when Nathan and the dogs left. What was happening here?

* * *

As Jessica wasn't coming, Nathan decided not to bother taking the car. He was in the mood for walking rather than driving. He took a familiar route past the spot where Jessica had been injured. He couldn't help glaring down at Dennis and Monty as they passed it. They'd caused a lot of trouble.

He was inordinately put out with his mum as well. Which was stupid, as it was his own fault she'd turned up out of the blue. He'd been having so much fun with Jessica, he hadn't even thought to charge his phone or check it.

He understood that his mum worried about him being on his own. Usually, he would have been glad to see her, but she hadn't exactly been subtle about not being happy to find Jessica there. She didn't even seem completely mollified when she found out their relationship was purely platonic. And he got why. She'd seen what he'd been through and had been there to pick up the pieces. But surely she must realise there was no way he'd get involved in a relationship now, and especially not with someone like Jessica whose whole life was her dancing and who lived on the other side of an ocean.

That hadn't stopped him from making that stupid comment about her pyjamas though, had it? He blushed just thinking about it. What an idiot. He hoped he hadn't come across as creepy. Maybe that was the reason Jessica hadn't wanted to come out. She'd hardly say she didn't want to come because he was being strange, would she? Should he apologise, or would that be making too much of the situation? He'd just have to see what the atmosphere was like when he got home. And he really must charge his phone.

* * *

Jessica was on the floor of the sitting room doing sit-ups when Nathan returned. Exercising was always the way she let out her stress.

"Hey," he said, putting his head around the door. Was it just her imagination, or was he looking at her strangely? As if guessing her thoughts, Nathan coughed and pulled his gaze away. "I'll put the dogs in the garden so they don't disturb you."

"Thanks."

Once the YouTube video she'd been doing came to an end, Jessica stood up. She knew she had to brave speaking to Nathan.

"How was your workout?" Nathan asked when she came into the kitchen.

"Good, thank you." Jessica helped herself to a glass of water. "Did you enjoy your walk?"

"Yeah. Monty was really good on the lead, and his recall is improving as well, thanks to cheese rewards."

"That's brilliant. The power of cheese, eh?"

Nathan's phone buzzed from where it was charging on the counter. He picked it up to check it.

"I had a message from my friend Stephen that I missed yesterday," he said. "He's another doctor at the surgery. He's inviting me to a barbecue at his house tonight. Says to bring a bottle and a guest. Do you fancy coming?"

"Erm . . ." Jessica looked for an excuse. Should she ask him about Claire? But if he'd wanted to tell her about Claire then presumably, he would have already. Maybe it was private. But if he did have a girlfriend, she wouldn't be too impressed with Jessica going to a barbecue with him.

"Look," said Nathan, shuffling uncomfortably. "I'm really sorry if my stupid comment about your pyjamas made you feel in any way uncomfortable. It was a daft thing to say."

"So, you don't like my pyjamas?" Jessica teased. It was funny to see him embarrassed.

"No, well, yes. I mean . . . you must know you look good in them."

Jessica arched an eyebrow.

"Well, you do . . . but I shouldn't have said anything."

"It's fine, honestly," said Jessica, laughing, glad that at least some of the tension between the two of them had gone. "Would you rather I didn't wear them anymore?"

"I'm pretty sure I can control myself," Nathan said drolly.

"Glad to hear it, because I don't think your mother would be too thrilled if you couldn't."

"You noticed . . ."

"Kind of hard not to."

"I'm sorry. She and I haven't been getting along all that well recently, and . . . basically, it's nothing to do with you."

82

"OK," said Jessica. If he had something he wanted to keep private, she needed to respect that. She supposed.

"Come to this barbecue with me, please? I really need to make some more friends around here, but I don't want to go by myself."

"I'm not sure I'm in the mood for loads of people . . ." Jessica was still feeling sorry for herself and the thought of having to explain to people why she was using crutches didn't particularly appeal.

"It won't be loads of people, and Stephen and his wife are really nice. Please?"

"All right, I'll come," she said. He was an adult and if he was in a relationship, it was his choice to invite her to come along, and it would probably do her good to go out for the evening. She couldn't hide away the whole time her foot was in plaster. "What time does it start?"

"Six. I'll message him that we're coming, and then I'll pop to the shops to get drinks for us to take with us."

"I should probably rest my foot up quite a bit before we go . . ."

"Yes . . . we can play some *Fable II*."

"Good. Hurry at the shops. I'll get us all set up."

CHAPTER EIGHT

"Be good, and we'll try not to be too late back," said Nathan seriously to Monty and Dennis.

"And don't do anything we wouldn't do," added Jessica, unsuccessfully attempting to divert her attention from her 'date' for the evening.

Nathan was wearing indigo jeans and a pale blue shirt rolled up to his elbows. He was fresh out of the shower, his hair still damp and smelling of grapefruit shampoo. Jessica couldn't stop her stomach from doing a little flip at the sight of him.

"You look lovely," Nathan said to her as they began the short walk to his friend's house. Jessica smiled; she'd put a lot of effort into her appearance this evening. The short floral dress she wore would have looked better with heels, but other than that, she was pleased with how she looked.

"I'm not convinced the crutches quite go with the outfit, but thanks."

"You're sure you don't want to go in the car?"

"We're almost halfway there now anyway, and you'll want to have a drink tonight. I'll be fine."

"OK, but I can always walk home and get the car to pick you up if you need me to. I'm not going to drink much, I've got work tomorrow," Nathan reassured her.

"Thanks. I'll bear that in mind. Have you been to Stephen's house before?"

"Just once."

"So, the friendship is still in the early stages."

"Very early stages," clarified Nathan. "Frankly, you're my secret weapon to increase my popularity."

"Oh, really?" replied Jessica. "You know I'm not very sociable?"

"Doesn't matter. I'm bringing a beautiful ballet dancer to the barbecue. I'm going to be the most popular guest there."

Jessica laughed. "An *injured* ballerina."

"That's even better: you have an air of tragedy about you."

"Weirdo."

"Just telling the truth."

Not many steps later, Nathan said, "Here we are." He indicated a grey terraced house with a dark blue door.

"Are you OK?" he asked. "You look a little stressed."

"Kind of," said Jessica. "Honestly, I'm not great at meeting new non-dance people for the first time."

"Seriously? But you dance in front of hundreds of people. I thought you'd be so confident."

"Nope! But I'm ready," she said. "Ring the doorbell. Anyone looking out will think we're nuts standing here on the doorstep chatting."

Nathan pressed the doorbell, and the door was opened by a tall man wearing shorts and a shirt covered in palm trees. His receding hairline gave away that he was a few years older than Nathan.

"Hey! I'm so glad you could come!"

"Wouldn't have missed it," replied Nathan. "Stephen, this is my friend, Jessica. Jessica, our host, Stephen."

"Hello," said Jessica with what she hoped was a charming smile. She really was feeling nervous now, which was daft because it was just a little barbecue, and she'd most likely never see these people again after this evening anyway.

"Come on through and grab a drink — everyone's in the garden."

The house was small and cosy, full of books, comfy chairs and knick-knacks. Jessica liked it immediately. The door to the garden was through the kitchen, and a few people were in there sorting out drinks.

"Hi, Nathan, thanks for coming," said a woman, giving him a kiss on the cheek.

Jessica bristled slightly despite herself, until Nathan said, "Jess, this is Stephen's wife, Amelia. Jessica's staying with me at the moment while her foot heals."

"I hope you're not stuck with him for too long," joked Amelia. "Doctors are the worst people to live with when you've got anything wrong with you."

Jessica laughed. "He's actually been brilliant — if a bit bossy."

Nathan threw her a look of mock indignation. "That's the thanks I get!"

"I said you'd been brilliant!"

"Can I get you both a drink before you end up falling out completely and leaving early?" asked Amelia.

"We brought some beers with us," said Nathan. "May I put them in the fridge?"

"If you can find room! There are some other people from the surgery outside."

"Excellent," he said. "Beer, Jess?"

"Sure."

He carried their drinks outside, where Jessica was grateful to see lots of available chairs.

A group of people called Nathan over, and they sat down in a couple of seats with them.

"So," said one man, eyeing up Jessica, "We finally get to meet Nathan's new girlfriend. We've been wondering why he's been running off home so quickly after work recently."

"Jess and I aren't together," Nathan said quickly.

"I'm just staying with Nathan for a while. We're old school friends," added Jessica.

"What did you do to your foot?" asked a small woman, who looked around Jessica's age.

"I was pushed over by my dad's unruly dog, and ended up breaking it."

"Oh no! And you're staying with Nathan while it heals?"

"Just for a while. I live in New York. I flew over here to surprise my family, but they were leaving to go on holiday, and then I broke my foot, and Nathan stepped in to help me out."

"What a hero." The woman looked over at Nathan. It was completely obvious that she fancied him and had been fishing for information about Jessica's relationship with him.

"He certainly is," said Jessica, automatically putting her hand on Nathan's knee. Why had she done that? She glanced at Nathan and saw that he was looking down at her hand. He looked up and caught her gaze. His hand covered hers and gave it a little squeeze. He didn't move it away.

What *is* happening here? thought Jessica. "What do you do in New York?" asked someone else.

"I'm a ballet dancer," Jessica said. She instantly had everyone's attention.

"Wow! Who do you dance with?"

"Are you with a company?"

"Where have you performed?"

The questions came thick and fast.

Nathan leaned closer to her, making her skin tingle. "Told you so," he whispered into her ear.

* * *

Three hours later and everyone had eaten. Jessica was stuffed full of king prawns, roasted vegetables and salad. The drinks had been flowing so well that people were now dancing. The group Jessica and Nathan had been part of had gradually gone to join the makeshift dance floor on the patio until only the two of them remained.

"Go and dance if you want to," said Jessica. "I'll be fine here by myself."

The song finished, and another slower one started.

"Dance with me," Nathan said.

Jessica stuck her plastered foot out to remind him of her predicament.

"You can just sway," he said, offering her his hand.

Jessica found herself putting her hand in his. She stood up and Nathan swept her into his arms.

"Oh . . ." Her memory of him carrying her before had been right. It had been a very nice experience.

Nathan walked with her into the centre of the dance floor and placed Jessica down carefully.

"Wow." Jessica gulped. "A girl could get used to this kind of treatment."

Her eyes met his. His gaze was intense, his dark pupils dilated.

She reached up and put her hands around Nathan's neck. She felt his hands on her waist and rested her head on his chest. Maybe she shouldn't have had the couple of beers she'd been enjoying during the evening. Should she break away? She could say her foot was hurting. That would be the perfect excuse to stop whatever it was they were doing here.

They moved in silence together, their bodies as close as it was possible to get them.

Nathan bent his head down. "Are you all right?" he whispered.

This was her chance to break away without anyone's feelings being hurt. They could just pretend nothing had happened. He knew she loved to dance, and had presumably thought she might like to try to join in with everyone else. It was a friendly thing to offer, but she could claim it had made her foot ache, and so had to be abandoned. No big deal.

Instead, Jessica nodded. She lifted her head and her eyes met Nathan's again. And suddenly his lips were on hers. Achingly gentle, tentatively exploring. He tightened his hold as she gave into her desire for him and their kiss deepened.

Then the song stopped and Pink's "Get the Party Started" began playing and their moment was over. Someone bumped into Jessica and apologised. Nathan steadied her.

Jessica reluctantly broke apart from him.

"I think I'd better sit this one out," she said. Her cheeks felt like they were on fire.

She half expected Nathan to pick her up again, but he didn't, though he did offer her his arm to aid her in hobbling back to her chair.

What had she been thinking kissing Nathan? She was going back to New York in a week and a half, and she certainly didn't want a relationship — she didn't have time for a relationship for one thing, even if there wasn't going to be an ocean separating them soon! And in front of all those people! That wasn't like her at all. What had come over her? Was she drunk? No, she'd only had two small beers, though she did feel rather light-headed now.

She had to admit, it had been a lovely kiss. She'd never been kissed like that before, with that intensity, so she felt it throughout her whole body. But that didn't matter. Nothing could come of it. And they would both get hurt if they started something there couldn't possibly be any future in.

Thankfully, Nathan was called over to speak to someone on the other side of the garden, giving Jessica a chance to collect her thoughts.

She really valued her friendship with Nathan, and she didn't want to ruin that.

She looked over at him talking to his friend. He laughed and glanced over at her. She managed to give him a little smile in return. He was so good to her, so kind and thoughtful. He'd be an amazing boyfriend, though not for her. Why on earth had she gone and spoilt everything?

Another man had joined in the conversation with Nathan and his friend. Seizing her opportunity, Jessica grabbed her crutches and put her cross-body bag over herself. As quickly and unobtrusively as possible, she snuck into the house. The kitchen was empty. Checking over her shoulder that Nathan hadn't spotted her, she made her way along the hall and out of the front door onto the street.

She breathed a sigh of relief. She quickly messaged Nathan so he wouldn't worry: *My foot's done for the night. I'm heading back to yours.*

That should buy her some time to sort her head out and work out how to salvage her friendship with Nathan if that was even possible.

She'd only made it to the corner of the street when she heard, "Jess! Jess! Wait up."

She stopped and turned. She'd known deep down that he would come out to find her as soon as he read her message, and it wasn't like she could move particularly quickly.

"Are you all right?"

"I'm fine," she said. "Go back and enjoy the party."

"Don't be daft," Nathan said immediately. "Let's go home. I think we need to talk."

"OK, but you should go and say goodbye."

"Yes, I should."

"Would you say thank you from me? I'll meet you back home."

Nathan didn't look happy about her walking by herself, but the determined look on her face told him there was no point in arguing this one.

"OK, but you might at least like to take the house keys with you." He handed Jessica a set of keys, making her blush. She'd been so anxious to get away she hadn't even thought about how she'd get into the house. "I'll see you soon." He gave her arm a gentle goodbye squeeze and walked back towards the party.

* * *

Jessica received a hero's welcome from Monty and Dennis, but not even their wagging tails and the fact that she'd managed to keep her balance when they came bounding over to her could make her smile.

She couldn't believe that she'd given in to a stupid whim to kiss Nathan. The first time she'd ever managed a proper friendship with a man — in fact, one of the only proper friendships she'd ever had — and she'd gone and messed it up.

She went into the kitchen and put on the kettle, automatically taking out two mugs to make Nathan a drink as well.

She continued berating herself: she really couldn't have chosen anyone more unsuitable to make a pass at. Not only was he one of her only genuine friends, but he lived thousands of miles away from her, and, from the sounds of things, he already had some sort of a relationship going with whoever this Claire woman was. Plus, he knew absolutely nothing about ballet and the world she lived in. He'd never understand her unusual life.

She made two cups of tea. She never normally drank the stuff, but she was in the mood for something comforting, and tea seemed to fit the bill. Anyway, wasn't tea what British people traditionally drank when they had a problem?

Nathan knocked on the door as she was finishing making the drinks.

"Thanks," he said when she let him in.

"Only you would say thank you to someone for opening your own front door to you," said Jessica. As much as she didn't want to have the conversation that was coming, she knew they had to. "Come into the kitchen, I've made you a cup of tea."

They sat opposite each other at the table.

"So . . ." Nathan began.

"Yeah . . ."

"I don't think either of us planned for that to happen."

"No," agreed Jessica. "The beer, and the party atmosphere . . ."

"Exactly. I'm sorry I overstepped the mark."

"Me too."

"I really don't want this to make things weird between us."

"Me neither, but if it is, and you'd rather I went back to my mum and dad's house, I can. I'm moving around much better now," said Jessica.

"No," replied Nathan immediately. "Please don't go because of this. I've . . . really enjoyed having you here, and I want you to stay until your parents come back. You still wouldn't be able to walk Monty by yourself. But of course, if you don't feel comfortable staying here . . ."

"No, it's not that! It's just that well . . . Claire," said Jessica awkwardly.

"Claire?" said Nathan, looking surprised.

"Yeah," said Jessica, embarrassed and wishing she hadn't brought the subject up. It was Nathan's business, and if he'd wanted to talk about it then he would have. But he'd sort of made it her business when he'd kissed her. "I overheard your mum asking what Claire would think about me staying here, so I'm guessing she's your girlfriend . . . partner . . . ?"

"She's my wife," said Nathan. "Well, ex-wife as of next week."

"Oh." Nathan was married? That wasn't something Jessica had even considered. He certainly didn't go around acting like someone who was married, well, separated, and very nearly divorced.

"I'm not very good at talking about it," Nathan explained. "But we'll be divorced in a few days. I only didn't mention her because I really don't like discussing her. I was having a good time with you, and it was nice not to be thinking about the divorce or the stupid decisions I've made in my life."

"I'm sorry . . ."

"It's not your fault, and I would have told you at some point. There just didn't seem to be any need to yet."

"So you definitely aren't in a relationship, then?" asked Jessica. At least she didn't need to feel guilty about stealing another woman's bloke that way.

"No," Nathan said. He took a deep breath. "Honestly, I still find it hard to imagine being in a relationship again.

My marriage ending was pretty brutal." He took Jessica's hand. "I'm really sorry. I shouldn't have kissed you tonight. It wasn't fair of me."

"I kissed you just as much as you kissed me," she said, which brought a smile to Nathan's face.

"Yes, you did," he said. She could swear he was blushing.

"But I'm going home to New York. You're an amazing guy but . . ."

"It's not the right time to start something between us," Nathan finished for her.

"Exactly. If things were different . . ."

"But they're not."

"Do you think we can go back to just being friends?" Jessica asked.

"I would love that," Nathan said, coming over to give her a hug. Jessica couldn't help breathing in some of his scent. "I've never had such a hot friend," he whispered into her hair.

Jessica laughed. "I definitely have. Loads of them in fact," she teased.

"You should have no trouble keeping your hands off me, then."

"No trouble at all." They held eye contact for a shade too long before Jessica broke away.

"So now that I know about Claire, do you want to talk about her? It might help," she asked, hoping to change the subject from the two of them.

"Maybe another time," Nathan said, his face clouding.

"OK, I'm always available if you need to chat."

"That's good to know."

"I think I might have an early night," she said. "It's been an eventful evening."

"It certainly has. See you tomorrow."

"Yeah, see you tomorrow."

Nathan gave her a tiny kiss on her forehead. "I'll let the dogs out and then I'll join you," he said, then quickly backtracked, "In having an early night, I mean, not actually joining you."

Jessica laughed. "Don't worry. I know what you meant." She couldn't stop herself giving Nathan a flirtatious wink before leaving the room.

* * *

What Jessica discovered over the next few days was that kissing Nathan at the barbecue had changed her relationship with him, but not in the way she'd thought it would. Acknowledging they were attracted to one another meant that they both felt free to show it, safe in the knowledge that they knew their flirtation wouldn't lead anywhere. This probably wasn't the best of ideas, but Jessica loved spending time with Nathan, and doing so made her feel good about herself at a time when she would have been pretty low without him around. It was nice to be desired even when she was hobbling around on crutches.

However, she could tell there was a definite change in mood when Nathan came home at lunchtime on Thursday to walk the dogs.

"Is today the day?" she asked, as he sat silently eating the lentil salad she'd made them.

"Yep. As of four o'clock this afternoon, I am officially divorced."

"I'm sorry."

"Thanks. And I'm sorry I'm not better company," he said. "I guess I'm just feeling a bit bleurgh."

"Completely understandable. Do you want to go out this evening and we'll see if we can't cheer you up?"

"I'd rather stay in, if you don't mind."

"Would you also rather I made myself scarce so you can brood by yourself?"

"No." Jessica was pleased to see that she'd managed to raise a very small smile from him. "I'd like to hang out with you, if that's all right, and if you're not sick of the sight of my miserable face."

"That is absolutely all right. Why don't I make us a curry and we could watch a film or something?"

"You'd give up a night of *Fable II* for me?"

"I would," Jessica stated solemnly. "But if you did want to play for a bit . . ."

* * *

Once Nathan had left to go back to work, Jessica put plan 'Cheer Nathan Up' into action. She found a rucksack in the cupboard under the stairs which she shrugged on.

"I'll be back soon, guys," she told Monty and Dennis. "Look after the place while I'm gone."

She'd walk to the supermarket and pick up the ingredients to make Nathan his special dinner. If her foot was aching a lot, she'd take a taxi back.

Jessica was walking along the main road through Bowerbridge, marvelling at how many of the shops she remembered from her childhood were still in business when she spotted a familiar tiny, straight-backed figure with a neat chestnut bob walking towards her.

"Madame Penny!" Jessica called out.

The figure looked up. "Jessica Stone! Well, I never. How lovely to see you. And please call me Diana," said her old ballet teacher, her face lighting up at the sight of her former pupil. "But what have you done to your foot?"

"I broke it soon after I arrived here to visit Mum and Dad."

"How long until it's fully healed?" asked Diana kindly, immediately understanding what the injury meant for Jessica.

Out of nowhere, tears sprang into Jessica's eyes and she found she was crying. She wiped them away, frustratedly. She'd been doing such a good job of holding her emotions in check and focusing on her recovery.

"Oh, you poor darling," said Diana, immediately putting her arms around her. "I was on my way to the dance studio, but I don't have a class for nearly an hour. Why don't you come with me and we can have a chat and a cup of tea?"

Jessica nodded her head, looking around to check there was no one watching her. She had never been the sort of person to burst into tears in the middle of the street! But then she'd had a huge disappointment and a lot of worry about her foot. Being with Nathan had taken her mind off her predicament brilliantly, but it hadn't changed the fact that her beloved career was very definitely in jeopardy.

She walked alongside Diana for the short distance to the dance studio — a building Jessica must have spent hundreds if not thousands of hours in when she was a child, but which she hadn't stepped foot in for about fifteen years.

Tears still stained her cheeks, but she smiled as she passed through the familiar double doors and into the large hall. The same piano stood in the corner, with probably the same CD player on top.

"Do you mind if I use the loo?" she asked, wanting to have a chance to wipe her eyes.

"Of course not. I'll pop the kettle on. Come and find me in the kitchen when you're done."

When Jessica emerged, tear stains removed, she realised she'd never been in the studio's kitchens before; it made her feel strangely grown up to be invited in there now. As it happened, it wasn't a very exciting room — just a galley kitchen, really, with a couple of stools next to one of the countertops.

"Here you go," said Diana, bringing two steaming mugs over to the stools. "I wasn't sure how you took your tea so I left it black, but there's milk and sugar if you like."

"Thank you. Black is fine." Jessica hid a grimace that she was once again drinking tea.

"Are you OK sitting on a stool with your foot?" Diana asked.

"Yes, thanks," said Jessica, resting her crutches against the counter and getting up onto the stool as gracefully as possible. She wished Nathan were there to give her a helping hand.

"So," Diana said, cutting straight to the point, "do you know how long this break is going to put you out of action for?"

"Three to six months," said Jessica. "I'm hoping to be able to start gentle training after three, depending on what more X-rays show."

"But the doctors think it will heal cleanly?"

"Hopefully. The X-rays weren't as clear as they'd like, though, and they said there looked like there was some previous damage."

"That's hardly unusual given your line of work, is it?"

"Exactly."

"I'm not surprised you're upset," said Diana, honestly.

"I'd just landed my first principal role," said Jessica. "It couldn't have come at a worse time."

"That really is terrible timing. What have your company said?"

"Not a lot, really. I called them when it first happened and they sorted out an insurance payment for me straight away, which was great. And I also spoke to my friend, who took over my role. But since then, I haven't heard from anyone."

"I would definitely make sure you keep them in the loop," Diana said. "Ballet can be a fickle business."

"I know," said Jessica. "Especially when you're not sure exactly when you're going to be able to perform again. Or if." She started crying again. Diana handed her a piece of kitchen roll.

"Have you been exercising?" she asked.

"Yes, I've still got to be really careful with my foot, but I've been exercising for at least a couple of hours every day."

"And have you got a good physiotherapist? A dancer-trained one?"

"Not at the moment," Jessica admitted. "Hopefully I will once I'm back in New York, but the insurance won't cover physio over here."

"It's still early days for that," said Diana. "Look, you are the most talented dancer I have ever been lucky enough to teach. And as well as that you're the most determined. If anyone can work hard enough to get her foot back to full strength, it's you."

"Thank you."

"Why don't you come along to my ballet class on Saturday morning?" Diana suggested. "You can help me with it. I'm a bit over-run at the moment. And I think it will do you good to be surrounded by other people who love ballet as you do."

"Thank you, I think that would be really helpful. I do feel a bit like a duck out of water here. No one understands how much ballet means to me. My family have always seen it as just a job."

"It's impossible to understand unless you have what I call the ballet gene," said Diana. "They don't mean to be unkind, it's simply not in them to feel so deeply about it."

"That's exactly it," said Jessica.

"And I remember your parents being hugely supportive of you."

"They were. They never complained about driving me to random places and hanging around for hours waiting for me."

"Your mother was so upset when you wanted to apply to ballet school. She came to talk to me about it," said Diana.

"I never knew that."

"She asked me not to say anything at the time. She was worried you were too young to be going away and that you'd regret focusing so much on one thing."

"And what did you tell her?" asked Jessica.

"I told her that you were hugely talented and that it would be an enormous waste not to nurture that talent. I also told her that if it all went pear-shaped, you'd still be so young that you could easily turn to something else, but that I thought she ought to let you give it your all."

"That's good advice."

"It's advice that still stands now," said Diana gently.

"You mean if my foot doesn't heal properly?" Jessica asked.

"Yes," Diana replied honestly.

"Thank you, Diana," said Jessica. "It's been really good to talk to you."

"It's been my pleasure. I'll see you on Saturday at ten."

"I'll be there."

* * *

98

Jessica left the dance studio feeling lighter than she had since before she'd had her accident. She wasn't sure she'd even been fully aware of the weight she'd been carrying around with her, but it had felt so good to be able to talk to someone who properly understood how she felt.

She walked to the supermarket more determined than ever to do something nice for Nathan. He'd been so kind to her, and he'd been hiding his own hurt which he hadn't felt able to talk about, even though he was always willing to listen to her going on about her problems. She wanted to try to help him like he'd tried to help her.

With her cooking really not being up to much, she picked up a jar of curry sauce and some chicken breasts. She grabbed a pot of microwavable basmati rice; she had a long history of burning rice and that gave her the best chance of not doing so tonight. She also got a bag of watercress and a tub of plain yoghurt and cucumber to make some raita. He'd want some poppadoms, she figured, so she got some of those and a jar of mango chutney. On the way to the till, she picked up a six-pack of Stella Artois on impulse.

She regretted her purchase of the beers within about a minute of leaving the supermarket. They were stupidly heavy in her rucksack. Still, it wasn't far to get home and she'd probably have to wait for ages for a taxi to arrive. Plus, it was a nice day and it felt good to be out, even if she was stuck on crutches.

When she got back to Nathan's house she still had almost two hours before he'd be home so she set to work making the place look nice. Despite her best efforts to be tidy, her stuff was still dotted around everywhere making the house look a mess. She picked it all up and put it in her room. She should really give that a good tidy-up as well, but that would have to wait for another day.

The sitting room was easy to dust because there was so little stuff in it, Nathan didn't really have knick-knacks. Hoovering with a foot in plaster wasn't at all easy, but the place definitely looked better once she'd finished. The back door had been open to air the downstairs, but Jessica took the dog beds outside and gave them a bash to remove the worst of the hair. Monty and Dennis eyed her very suspiciously while she did this.

Next, she prepared the kitchen, emptying the dishwasher and wiping down all the countertops and the table. She laid the table ready for their dinner. She hesitated when she went to add candles — would they come across as too romantic? But she wanted to make the table special for him.

She stepped back and surveyed her work: it looked good. It was as neat and tidy as when she'd first arrived. She really must do better about keeping her stuff in her room.

All the moving around had made her foot ache more, so she grabbed a book and went to sit out in the garden in the sun with the dogs until Nathan got back from work.

* * *

"What's happened here? Have we been robbed?" said Nathan with mock horror as he came in the front door.

"I tidied up!" declared Jessica, proudly. "Doesn't it look great? Your space is once again free from all my stuff!"

"That was really nice of you," Nathan gave Jessica a hug. "But I like your stuff around."

"Really? But you're so tidy. I thought it must be driving you crazy."

"It makes the house feel more like a home," said Nathan with a shrug.

"Well, I shall endeavour to mess it all up again very soon."

"I'd appreciate that."

"How are you feeling?" Jessica asked.

"OK, I guess. I had a message from my solicitor to say that everything went through fine. I am officially divorced, which is a good thing, I suppose."

"Let's take your mind off things," suggested Jessica. "Do you want to take the dogs out? If we drove to the playing fields, I should be able to hobble around them on my crutches."

"Sure, some sun and fresh air will do me good."

* * *

When they returned to the house an hour later, Nathan did seem to be in a happier mood.

"I'm taking over this evening now," said Jessica, bossily. "I'd like you to go upstairs and change out of those sensible work clothes and into something comfortable and ideally with an elasticated waist."

"Right-o," said Nathan.

Jessica began cutting up the chicken breast, wishing she'd brought the strips so she didn't have to handle the poultry as much.

"Well, I never," said Nathan, coming up behind her. "I never thought I would see you chopping up raw meat."

"Don't get used to it," grumbled Jessica. "This is a special occasion."

"You mean you'll only cook for me when I get divorced?"

"Yes. There are cold beers in the fridge, so grab yourself one and stick some music on, then you can chat and entertain me while I slave away at the cooker top."

"I'm not going to argue with that," he said. "A beer for you too?"

"I think I'm going to need one."

Jessica began frying the chicken and diced up some onion and some peppers which she added to the pan once the chicken was cooked through.

"If you give me food poisoning, I may never forgive you," said Nathan, placing her drink beside her.

"If you keep on complaining, you won't get any supper," Jessica retorted.

"That might be safer, to be honest. You did use a different knife and board for the chicken and the vegetables, didn't you?"

"I used a different knife and turned the board over. Stop fussing."

"I didn't realise being concerned about salmonella was fussing."

"It is. Drink your beer."

She looked over her shoulder at Nathan and threw him a smile.

"You are incorrigible," he said, but he smiled back. "Are you sure you're OK standing there to cook?"

"If I say I'm not, will you come and take over?"

"Probably. It seems I'm a soft touch when it comes to you."

"I've noticed that too, but I'm fine, honestly, and I can leave it and sit down in a minute anyway." She turned back to the food but could feel Nathan's eyes on her, checking she really was fine standing.

"Thank you for doing this for me," he said.

"Don't be daft." Jessica added the sauce to the pan. "You've cooked for me loads, it's nothing."

She turned the curry down to simmer and joined Nathan at the table.

"It's nice to be able to do something for you for a change," she said.

"I have to say, the food does smell really yummy."

"Of course it does. Not even I could mess this up."

* * *

Even so, Jessica was surprised to discover their supper was edible. After the meal, she offered to clean up by herself, but Nathan insisted on helping. "I've eaten so much, I need to move about to help me digest."

"That's your medical opinion, is it?"

"Yes, and I'm standing by it."

It took longer than usual for the kitchen to be cleared; Jessica was a far messier cook than Nathan, it seemed. "I'm not going to ask how you managed to get bits of chopped onion as far as the hallway," Nathan commented, before suggesting, "Another beer?"

"Why not?"

"Let's take them outside. Come on, boys." Nathan whistled and the dogs followed him into the garden.

"How are you doing?" asked Jessica, accepting a drink from him.

"OK." He sat down heavily in a plastic chair. "It's definitely for the best, but it's strange that my marriage is now officially over, even though we've been apart for over a year."

"What made you choose Bowerbridge to move to?" asked Jessica, carefully.

"To begin with, I tried to stay in Manchester. I liked my job and I had friends there, but most of my friends were Claire's friends as well, and it got kind of awkward. I think I needed to make a proper break. I started to look around for another job and it seemed a little bit like fate that one showed up in Bowerbridge. I have such happy memories here, and it's close to my mum and my sister now. My sister's a nurse in Tonbridge and my mum moved to be close to her when my eldest niece was born."

"And did having a proper break work?"

"It's helped, especially getting Dennis."

"He's very good company."

"He certainly is. And I like that it's quiet here and that I've been largely left alone to brood, but having you to stay has made me see that I need to have other people around me again, outside of work."

"It can't be easy having your marriage end," Jessica said, putting her hand on his.

"And this was technically my second marriage," Nathan said.

"You've been married before?" said Jessica, struggling to keep the shock from her voice. How had two women been stupid enough to let Nathan go?

"You of all people should know that," Nathan said, a grin forming on his lips.

Seeing her perplexed look, he continued, "We were married one playtime when we were in Year 1. Ryan Thomas was my best man, and you had about ten bridesmaids. I can't believe you don't remember."

Jessica laughed. "You really had me going there! I think I do remember actually — you said we had to do it quickly because you needed to get back to your football match."

"Ever the gentleman." Nathan gave a little bow. "If I recall, the game had carried on from the day before, so was of vast importance."

"More important than your bride?"

"What can I say? I was young and an idiot. Any man would have to be to let you slip through his fingers."

Nathan's gaze met Jessica's and drifted down to rest on her mouth. Jessica swallowed hard as neither of them broke the silence.

"It's a good thing we've both decided not to do any more kissing," she said, managing to find her voice. "Otherwise I think we could be in trouble here."

"Yeah," said Nathan, throatily. "Definitely a good thing."

It took all of Jessica's self-control to stand up. "Come on, let's go and play *Fable II*. There's some weird quest where you have to throw a chicken at a magic door that I want to complete."

"Only if I get ice cream," said Nathan. "I think I've got a tub of Ben and Jerry's in the freezer."

"I'll get the Xbox fired up," Jessica said.

That was a close one, she thought to herself as she headed back inside. It was taking a lot of willpower not to give in and kiss Nathan again, but it was for the best, especially with him only just divorced and her going back to New York soon. She'd never want to hurt him, and if he liked her half as much as she liked him, that's exactly what would happen if she gave in to her feelings for him.

CHAPTER NINE

"I can't believe your family is coming back tomorrow and this is your last full day here," said Nathan, when Jessica came out into the kitchen for her breakfast on Saturday morning. "It's going to be so quiet without you and Monty around."

"I'm not going back to the States for a few more days, so you won't get rid of us completely," Jessica reminded him.

"No, but it won't be the same, so we need to make today special. What would you like to do? I'm at your disposal."

"I actually have a prior engagement, but only for part of the morning. I said to my old ballet teacher that I'd drop in and give her a hand with a class at ten. It's only an hour, I think."

"That'll be nice for you. Make sure you don't overdo it, though. You should still be keeping off that foot as much as possible."

"I know, don't worry, Dr Townsend."

"How about I pick you up afterwards and we can do something?"

"Sure. What did you have in mind?"

"I've got an idea, but I'm not telling you what it is."

"Intriguing . . ."

"And actually, you being out for a while will give me time to organise it."

"How mysterious! I love it!"

"Would you like a lift to the dance studio?"

"No, thanks. The walk will be good exercise. Will what I'm wearing be OK for whatever you have planned?"

"Yeah, it should be fine, just don't change into a tutu during class."

Seeing Jessica's face fall, Nathan quickly said, "I'm so sorry. That was really thoughtless of me." He wrapped her in a hug, pulling her close to him.

"It's fine," she said, determined to pull herself together. "I'm just still a bit sensitive about not being able to dance."

"Of course you are. That was a completely stupid thing for me to say."

"Don't worry. I'm sure I'll say something daft to you later about ex-wives and then we'll be even."

"You make sure you do," Nathan said, giving her a kiss on the head and letting her go.

"I'd better get ready," Jessica said.

"I'll be going out in a minute, so I'll see you outside the dance studio at eleven."

"Sounds good." She stood on tiptoe and kissed Nathan on the cheek. "See you then." Their eyes met and held for a beat before Jessica reluctantly broke her gaze.

* * *

Jessica was glad to be by herself for a little while before the class. She knew that she'd find it hard watching all the students dancing and not being able to join in, but at least this class was for little ones who wouldn't be going through all the familiar routines she knew and loved. She also knew that it was important she did this. It was going to be three months at least until she'd be able to begin training again; she needed things to fill up her time or she'd go crazy counting down the days until her life could begin again. Not being able to dance had made it completely plain to her just how much of her life ballet was, and how lacking it was in many ways without it. Maybe teaching could be what she needed at the moment, and it might even be her future.

She packed a bag, just like she always would for class, but without her dance shoes and leotard, which definitely felt strange.

She made sure that she was at the dance studio ten minutes early. None of the students had arrived yet, but Diana was there putting music ready in the CD player.

"Please say that's the same CD you used to play when I first started coming here," said Jessica.

"The very same!" Diana laughed. "But I have upgraded the player."

"Wonderful!"

"I've put a chair for you by the piano. Would you be able to stop and start the music for me when I ask?"

"No problem," Jessica said as cheerfully as she could.

"Don't worry," said Diana quickly. "That's not all I want you to do! Could you also be an extra set of eyes for me and, if you're up to it, you could walk around the class, making any corrections as you see fit."

"Of course." Jessica was much happier now she realised she would have a proper job to do.

The children began to arrive, all aged between four and six, just like Jessica when she started. They were mostly little girls, but Jessica was pleased to see a couple of boys as well. It was important to get them when they were young so their love for ballet could develop before they were told that it wasn't cool for them to dance and got put off.

There was mayhem as children got ready and then ran around, parents dropping them off, some wanting to speak to Diana, but as soon as it was ten o'clock, Diana said, firmly, "OK children, into position!"

Fifteen sets of tiny feet hurried to get into place in three lines of five.

"I'd like to introduce you to my helper for today, Jessica. Jessica is a professional ballerina. She's hurt her foot so can't dance at the moment, but she's very kindly offered to give us a hand."

Jessica felt fifteen pairs of eyes turn to her, several of them wide with admiration.

"I'm sure you've got lots of questions for Jessica, but that will have to wait until after class. Jessica, could you start the music, please?"

* * *

The class flew by. The children were very sweet and listened earnestly whenever Jessica came over to help or correct them. The music reinforced all of her happy memories of when she'd first started dancing. How she used to be so impatient to get to class that she'd run the whole way, and would always be the first one there. She wondered if any of these children felt the same way. They were so young, it was impossible to tell if they had the talent, the drive and the body shape to become a professional.

She'd been so engrossed in the class, that it was only when the children had all left and she was saying goodbye to Diana that she remembered Nathan was picking her up and they were going out on their mystery outing together.

Nathan was waiting in his Land Rover outside the studio. The car had a large green Canadian canoe tied firmly onto the roof rack.

"Hi!" said Nathan cheerfully, getting out to greet her and help her into the car like he always did.

"You want me to go canoeing with a broken foot? What if I fall in? I'm not supposed to get the plaster wet."

"You won't fall in. The canoe is really stable, and we're going to be going on the canal so the water's completely calm."

"There's a canal near here?"

"Yeah, well, not that far away. It's near Guildford. The canal's also handy because you can just turn around and paddle back to the car without having to go against a current."

"And you're sure I won't end up in the water?"

108

"I'm positive."

Choosing to trust Nathan against her better judgement, Jessica got in the car. She checked the back seats. "Aren't the dogs coming with us?"

"No. Monty in a canoe would be a recipe for you getting a dunking. I've given them both a bit of a walk and they've got the run of the garden."

* * *

They pulled into a parking space by the canal an hour later. Jessica eyed the water suspiciously. It looked cold.

Nathan helped her out of the car. "I'll get the canoe off the roof," he said. "There's a buoyancy aid for you in the boat. It's the red one."

"If I'm definitely not going to fall in, then why do I need a buoyancy aid?"

"For safety, and so that I can get photos of you wearing one."

Muttering darkly to herself, Jessica put on the buoyancy aid. It smelled mildewy. How did she let herself get talked into these things?

Nathan joined her and put on his own blue version.

"I hate you right now," said Jessica.

"Come on, let's get this boat in the water," he said, ignoring her.

Nathan pulled the canoe over to the canal and gently eased it into the water before getting in himself. "Can you pass me that rucksack?" he asked, indicating a bag he'd left on the path.

Jessica handed it to him.

"OK, now, give me your hand, and I'll help you in."

Jessica very gingerly accepted his help and climbed into the canoe, managing to stifle a scream when the boat wobbled rather alarmingly as she did so.

She collapsed onto one of the benches and glared at Nathan.

"See, completely safe," he said, looking a little guilty.

"I'm not having a good time so far," Jessica said through gritted teeth.

"You will be soon," Nathan reassured her, handing her a wooden paddle.

"You expect me to paddle as well!" Jessica said incredulously.

"It'll be good exercise for your arm muscles."

"Fine," grumped Jessica, taking hold of the paddle.

It didn't take long for Jessica's bad mood to dissipate. Nathan was right; now that she was in it, the canoe was very stable. It was a glorious sunny day, the light hitting the water was beautiful, and the trees alongside the canal afforded them much-needed shade. The ducks and swans passing by provided some entertainment, as did the people travelling along the towpath. And it was nice to be outside doing something vaguely physical which didn't involve using crutches.

Jessica smiled and turned her face to catch the sun. "I knew you'd enjoy it," she heard Nathan comment quietly.

They paddled for about an hour with Nathan at the back of the canoe steering, pointing out things to one another. It was so peaceful and relaxing and they were going at such a lazy pace that Jessica didn't think her arms were getting much of a workout, though she'd probably have blisters on her hands from holding the paddle.

"Shall we stop for lunch?" asked Nathan. "There's a good point where we can moor up just ahead."

"That sounds good." Jessica's busy morning meant she was very hungry.

Nathan directed them to a spot with an easy exit point.

"Are you all right getting out of the canoe for lunch? We can stay in it if you'd rather but there's a nice spot for a picnic on the grass over there."

"I'll be brave."

Nathan stepped out first and tied the canoe up on a mooring, and then helped Jessica out and retrieved her crutches from the bottom of the canoe as well as his rucksack. "It's just over there." He pointed to a grassy area underneath a large oak tree.

They walked over and Nathan unpacked the rucksack to reveal a picnic rug and several containers of food. "Are you OK sitting on the ground?" he asked. "Otherwise, I think there's a bench we can move to a little further along the towpath."

"I'll be fine if you can just give me a hand getting down."

Once she was settled on the rug, Nathan began unpacking Tupperware. He'd brought cheese, salami and olives, as well as a rice salad, hummus and falafels — basically all Jessica's favourite picnic food. There was also a large tub of strawberries.

"Thank you so much," said Jessica tucking in. "This all looks delicious."

"My pleasure." He handed her a bottle of water. "There's also a flask of coffee and some granola bars, but I thought we could save those for later."

"Sounds like a good plan."

"So, are you having an OK time?" Nathan asked with a grin.

"I am," Jessica admitted. "This was a really lovely idea."

"I'm glad. It's going to be really strange not having you around all the time. And Monty, of course."

"But I'm sure it'll be nice to have your home back to yourself. You'll be able to walk around naked, or whatever it is you like to do when you're alone."

Nathan laughed. "I don't think poor Dennis deserves to put up with that kind of behaviour." He ate a piece of salami, then continued, "To be honest, I thought I would struggle having a guest. I've lived by myself for a while now, and you saw how tidy I kept things. I wasn't sure how well I'd cope with my routine being changed, but I've really loved having you. It's been nice to have someone to come home to in the evenings."

"I'm glad I wasn't too much of a pain. I know I can be kind of messy," Jessica admitted.

"You really can!" Nathan chuckled. "But I liked it. I think it's the first time that house has felt like a home. I'm going to need to do something about that. Though I'm not sure what exactly."

"Maybe you need more stuff around. It does feel a little like a show home . . . Sorry," she said, seeing Nathan wince.

"No, you're right. It does. Claire got most of the furniture in the divorce, so I just bought whatever I needed from IKEA."

"Well, you won't get rid of me easily. I'm sure I'll be popping around to make a mess before I fly back to the States."

"You'd better," said Nathan, smiling, though there was a sad look in his eyes.

Jessica shimmied over to be closer to him. "Thank you so, so much for the last week and a half. It's meant so much to me. Not just because I would have struggled physically by myself, but because you really cheered me up. I can't believe I've actually enjoyed myself in the depths of my despair."

"And thank you for cheering me up on Thursday. I'd probably still be wallowing now if it weren't for you." He gave her a hug.

"We make quite a team," Jessica said.

"That we do," agreed Nathan. "Let's take a photo. I want to remember this."

"No way am I being photographed dressed in this!"

"Just one, please? I won't show it to anyone."

"All right, just one," she agreed.

They leaned close together and Nathan used his phone to take a selfie.

"Look, it's really nice," he said, showing her the image.

"I suppose it's not terrible," Jessica admitted. Actually, it was a lovely photograph. Jessica was used to having her picture taken for work, both while she was dancing and for headshots and the occasional magazine or newspaper article about her or her company. These photos were always very staged, and she had time to ensure that she looked absolutely perfect for them. But in this quick snap taken with her hair a mess from the wind and without a scrap of make-up on her face, she looked really happy. She and Nathan fitted well together. They looked like a couple. The kind of couple other couples aspired to be, having fun adventures on the weekend and enjoying each other's company in the outdoors.

* * *

They lazed around for a while after they'd finished eating, debating how much further they would travel before turning back. They decided to go for another hour, stop again and have their coffee and snack, and then head back.

The sky clouded over while they were paddling. Jessica insisted on being at the back this time so she could have a turn steering. They chatted as they paddled, but not about anything important. It seemed they'd both decided they were taking an afternoon off from the troubles in their lives and were just going to enjoy being together.

It was almost five o'clock by the time they reached the landing stage where they'd first got into the canoe.

They performed their usual routine of Nathan getting out first and then helping Jessica to disembark. Once she was safely on dry land, Nathan went to step back into the canoe to retrieve their things, but he misjudged his step. His foot caught the edge of the canoe, pushing it away from the canal bank, and, before Jessica could do anything to stop him, Nathan landed in the water with a large splash.

"Oh no! Are you OK?" Jessica hurried over to the side of the canal.

"Yes," said Nathan, his head appearing out of the water. He stood up. The water only reached his stomach.

Jessica burst out laughing. "No chance of anyone falling in, eh?" she eventually managed to say.

"I think what I actually said was that there was no chance of *you* falling in, and in that regard, I was right," Nathan retorted, hauling himself into the canoe.

"I will never let you live this down," said Jessica, whipping out her phone and taking a photo of a very soggy Nathan.

* * *

Nathan got himself and the canoe out of the water and took off his soaking buoyancy aid — and T-shirt. His body wasn't as sculpted as those of the dancers Jessica knew, but he definitely kept in shape, and he looked strong and, somehow, safe.

"What are you staring at?" He laughed. "Your mouth is practically hanging open!"

"It is not!" said Jessica, blushing.

"You've got plenty more time to check me out," Nathan said. "I don't have another top to change into until we get home. Are there any particular poses you'd like me to hold?"

Jessica threw his damp T-shirt at him. "We'd better get you home as quickly as possible so you don't scare anyone."

Nathan helped Jessica into the Land Rover, a little smile playing on his lips, which Jessica decided to ignore. He didn't need any more encouragement. She couldn't help the occasional look over at his chest while he was driving, though.

CHAPTER TEN

"What time are you going to be heading off?" Nathan asked when he joined Jessica for breakfast the next morning. He'd already been out for a run and was fresh out of the shower. He smelled delicious.

"Mum and Dad are due mid-afternoon; I want to be there to meet them. I also thought I might go to the supermarket and pick up some food for them, so I'll probably need to head off after lunch."

"I've got nothing on, other than pining for you and Monty from after lunchtime onwards," Nathan said. "What if I drive you to the supermarket? I could do with doing a shop for me as well, and I can help you push the trolley around."

"That sounds nice." Jessica was so grateful to have a little more time with Nathan.

This last act of domesticity in the form of going to the supermarket together seemed to make the thought of leaving Nathan's home worse somehow. Jessica knew she wouldn't have any chance to be lonely while she was at her parents' house, but she would definitely miss Nathan and the easy camaraderie the pair of them shared. When she was with him, it always felt like there was someone on her side.

Jessica debated cooking for her parents to welcome them home, but, frankly, it was bound to go wrong, so she picked up a ready-made paella which just needed to be popped in the oven for half an hour. She also got a bunch of roses, her mum's favourite flower, to welcome them home, as well as basics like eggs, milk and bread.

They were loading up the boot of the Land Rover with all the shopping when Jessica heard her name being called. Turning, she saw Diana coming across the car park.

"Hi, Jessica," Diana said when she reached her. "I'm glad I caught you. I forgot to get your phone number yesterday after class."

"Oh, right, I'll pop it in your phone if you like." Diana handed Jessica her phone and Jessica tapped her number in.

"You must be the young man who's been looking after Jessica," Diana said, looking Nathan up and down. Jessica smiled, noticing the way her ballet teacher analysed everyone's physique out of habit, just like she did herself.

"I am," he said, shaking Diana's hand. "Not that she's been a very good patient."

"I don't think any injured ballet dancer makes a good patient," Diana said, laughing.

"Well, at least I know it's not just Jess, then," Nathan said with a grin.

"Jessica, while I've got you here," Diana said, "it was so helpful to have you as an extra pair of eyes yesterday, and the children seemed to like you very much. I was wondering if you could help me with another class, at five tomorrow evening? Only if your foot can handle it, of course."

"Um, yes, sure. That would be fun." It was nice to feel wanted for something dance-related and Jessica knew it was important she kept busy.

"Great, I'll see you tomorrow then," said Diana.

"For sure." Jessica waved goodbye as Diana continued into the supermarket.

"That sounds cool," Nathan said once Diana was out of earshot.

"Yeah, I enjoyed it yesterday. And I definitely think I need to be filling my time up while I can't dance."

"That's a lot of time to fill up."

"I know. It turns out I didn't really do very much apart from dance."

Nathan was silent.

"Are you OK?" Jessica asked. She'd expected him to make a kind comment like he usually did. Something along the lines of he was sure she had plenty of other things in her life, or that she'd had to spend so much time dancing so that she could be the best ballerina she could possibly be.

"Yeah, I'm fine," he said, quickly. "Let's get this food home before my ice cream melts."

* * *

Jessica's mum and dad were thrilled to find her waiting for them when they got home, although Jessica suspected that her dad was almost as pleased to be reunited with Monty, who he took out for a little walk within five minutes of arriving back. As sweet as Monty was, she breathed a sigh of relief that she was no longer in charge of him.

"How's your foot feeling? Is it very painful?" Sarah fussed. "You haven't been overdoing it, have you?"

"Don't worry, Mum. I've been really careful. It's not too sore, but it does ache more if I don't rest it regularly. And Nathan looked after me really well."

"Oh, yes. You and Nathan. What's going on there? He's very handsome."

"Yes, he is," admitted Jessica. There was no point in denying that; it was a fact. "But there's nothing going on between us, we're just friends."

Sarah's face showed that she wasn't convinced, but she said, "If you say so."

* * *

"Everyone's coming round for supper tonight at about six," Sarah told Jessica the next morning.

"Oh, great. I'm helping Madame Penny with a dance class, but I'll be home by about quarter past."

"Lovely. Would you like to invite Nathan?"

"Nathan?" Jessica asked, surprised.

"Yes, Nathan. The man who looked after you while we were away, remember. I'd like the chance to thank him."

"OK, I'll see if he's free."

Jessica didn't know how she felt about Nathan coming to her parents' house. Would it be strange for those two parts of her life to collide? Her mum would definitely be watching how she and Nathan were together. Well, she'd said she'd invite him, so she would. Maybe he wouldn't be free.

She typed: *Hi. My mum's asking if you'd like to come for supper tonight. The whole family's going to be here. Don't worry if you'd rather not.*

She read back over it. It didn't sound very friendly. But she didn't want him to feel obliged to come. Despite what he said about enjoying having her stay, he might be loving having his house back and being by himself. Or he might simply rather not spend an evening with her whole family. She sent it before she could overthink it anymore.

Almost immediately three dots appeared under the message as Nathan began replying. Then they disappeared. A moment later he started typing again, but once more stopped. Finally, after a third lot of dots, his message came through. *Sure, what time?*

I'm doing that dance class at 5. Meet me outside the studio just after 6 and we can walk to my mum and dad's house together?

Great. What should I bring?

Just yourself.

My mother always taught me to never go to dinner empty-handed.

You're always so polite. My mum and dad love chocolate.

OK. See you later. x

A kiss at the end of the message. Jessica smiled and decided not to overthink it.

* * *

118

The children attending this class were a little older, so there was more for Jessica to correct and note, which made helping out even more interesting. There were a couple of girls in the group who looked like they could be quite promising.

"That was brilliant," she said to Diana when all the children had left. "It's still hard to tell if any of them have real talent, but they seem to really love the class, and it was brilliant when Flora made that jump."

"It was. She was so proud of herself," Diana said. "You have a real talent for helping them. You're very observant, and I like the way you always comment when you see an improvement."

"Thank you. I've done some teaching before, during the months when my company's closed down for the summer, but because it was a summer school, the kids were never properly invested in the ballet. It was just another activity on offer for them to try, and because I didn't get to work with the same children for long, I never got to see them progress."

"It's a pity you won't be able to follow any of these children's progress either. Some of them have already made such strides since they started. When are you flying back?"

"Wednesday night."

"And how do you feel about that?"

"I don't know," Jessica said honestly. "I thought I'd be really pleased to get back, but I've hardly spent any time with my family with them being away."

"Could you stay for longer? I'd love to have you around to help me with more classes. But I insist upon paying you."

"Oh, thank you. That's a very kind offer. The extra money would be handy. Can I get back to you tomorrow?" answered Jessica. She hadn't for one moment expected her old dance teacher to want her at classes more regularly, had really thought she was just taking pity on her while she was in town. She was definitely tempted.

"Of course," Diana said, patting Jessica on her arm.

It was fair to say that Jessica had considered changing her flight for many reasons. She pushed the six-foot-two one out of her head . . . But what would she do with herself for longer in Bowerbridge? And she had a life to return to. But how much of that life was actually worth returning to when she wasn't able to dance? Getting up and down all the steps to her apartment would be a nightmare, even without trying to carry groceries up them. She knew her ballet colleagues would help if she asked, especially Bethany, but she didn't want them to see her like this. And her apartment would be fine without her for a while longer, she supposed.

If she stayed, she could spend some more time with her family and earn a bit of extra money while doing something useful with her time and seeing if teaching really was for her. Plus, there was Nathan . . .

* * *

"Hey, you," said Nathan when Jessica came out of the studio, a smile breaking over his face. He was leaning against a wall enjoying the early evening sunshine.

"Hi." Jessica smiled back. "Are you sure you want to do this?"

"Are your family really that terrible?"

"No, but my brother and his wife will be bringing their kids . . ."

"I like kids," Nathan said simply, with a shrug.

"Just don't say you weren't warned." They started walking. "How was your day?"

"It was good. Not too busy. How was yours?"

"It was nice. I hung out with Mum for the day. We went out for lunch and watched a film together this afternoon. I can't remember the last time I did something like that with her. Did you miss me and Monty last night?"

"Naturally. It wasn't the same playing *Fable II* without you."

"You played *Fable II* without me!" Jessica cried indignantly, ready to turn the full force of her wrath onto Nathan.

Nathan laughed. "Of course not, I'm just winding you up."

"Idiot," muttered Jessica.

They reached Jessica's parents' house. Jessica glanced at Nathan and thought he looked a little nervous. She gave his hand a squeeze.

Everyone was gathered in the kitchen and turned as one when Jessica and Nathan came in. They were greeted first by Monty, who acted like he hadn't seen Nathan for years, running in circles around him and bringing him every toy he owned.

"Everyone, this is Nathan," Jessica said. "Nathan, everyone."

A chorus of hellos rang out.

"I remember teaching you," Sarah said, coming over to welcome their guest.

"You were my favourite teacher, Mrs Stone," Nathan said.

Jessica audibly groaned. "You can dial down the charm, Nathan. She already likes you because you looked after me."

"I'm naturally charming," insisted Nathan. "I can't help it."

Sarah laughed. "And you know my husband and my son, Andrew."

"Of course," Nathan said. "Andrew once let me be goal-keeper for him and his friends during break time when I must have been about Year 3 and they were Year 5. It was the single greatest moment of my childhood."

"I imagine it must have been," said Andrew. "My friends and I all thought we were the coolest. Every one of us was going to end up playing for Man United. This is my wife, Molly, and our munchkins, Peter, Emily and Sophie."

Nathan smiled at Molly and then spoke to the children. "Do you like football like your dad?"

"Yeah," said all three at once.

"Do you want to see me do kick-ups?" asked Peter.

"Sure," Nathan said, prompting Peter to rush off with the cry, "I'll get my ball!"

"Not in the house," said Molly, quickly.

"Come out into the garden," said Sophie, pulling Nathan towards the back door.

"Is that all right?" Nathan asked around.

"Sure, if you don't mind," said Joe, busy preparing a salad. Nathan was dragged outside by the children.

"He's certainly very popular," said Sarah pointedly to her daughter. Jessica felt her cheeks flush. "You sit down, and rest that foot."

Jessica pulled out one of the kitchen chairs from under the table and settled herself on it. Her brother sat down next to her.

"Hey, sis." Andrew gave her a hug. "Sorry to hear about your foot."

"Yeah," said Molly. "Do you know when the plaster can come off?"

"Another four and a half weeks," Jessica said with a sigh. "Tell me all about your holiday," she added, hoping to turn the conversation away from her injury.

"It was really nice," Molly said, leaning against a work-top. "I think we managed to visit every tourist attraction within a thirty-mile radius of where we were staying. The kids were exhausted when we got back. They were not impressed at having to get up early this morning to go to holiday club so that Andrew and I could get back to work."

"How's the accountancy firm?" asked Jessica.

"Good. We actually took on another accountant a couple of months ago."

"That's brilliant."

Jessica chatted with her family for a few minutes and then thought she ought to go and check how Nathan was doing with the children.

When she went outside, she could immediately tell he was having a good time. A very intense game of two-a-side football was going on — Nathan and little Sophie, against Peter and Emily.

She smiled watching Nathan play with the children. He obviously really did love kids. Sensing someone was watching

him, Nathan looked up and smiled at Jessica. "Pay attention," said Sophie sternly.

"You sound just like your auntie when you speak to me
like that!" said Nathan, laughing.

* * *

Supper was a relaxed affair. Joe had cooked a load of chicken
drumsticks and sausages on the barbecue, and there was a
rice salad, a green salad, boiled potatoes, and bread. The table
practically groaned under the weight of the food.

The kitchen table wasn't big enough for nine, so a large
fold-up table had been set up in the garden for them all.

"It's so lovely to have everyone here all together," said
Sarah, as they took their places with full plates of food.

Jessica looked around at her family. Her dad gave her
mum a kiss. Andrew was helping Sophie cut up her food
while Molly refereed between Peter and Emily who were trying to see which of them would be brave enough to eat an
olive. Finally, her gaze fell on Nathan, and their eyes met. He
was so lovely and kind playing with her nieces and nephew.
He gave her a wink and turned to answer a question her
dad had asked him. She needed more of this in her life, she
realised. More time with people she loved and who loved her
and genuinely cared about her because of who she was, not
because of how well she could dance. How could she have
been so blasé about seeing her family? Yes, there had certainly been plenty of times when she'd needed to work and
couldn't fly over to visit, but there had also been occasions
when she could have made more of an effort. And maybe it
would have done her good to have stepped out of her little
ballet bubble once in a while. But at least she was here now,
she told herself, properly appreciating what she had.

"Everyone," she said to get people's attention, "I have
something to ask."

Everybody stopped talking. "Madame Penny says she'd
like me to help out more with her classes, as a paid assistant,

so I was wondering if it would be all right for me to stay for a bit longer. At least until my cast is off."

"Of course it is!" Sarah said, not even attempting to hide how delighted she was.

"Does that mean I can go to dance class with you?" asked Emily.

"If that's all right with your mum and dad," said Jessica.

"I'm sure we can sort that out," Molly said with a smile, prompting an excited squeal from Emily.

"This is excellent news!" exclaimed Joe. "I'm going to get some bubbles out of the fridge to celebrate with!"

Finally, Jessica dared to turn to see Nathan's reaction. He nodded and gave her a little smile which didn't seem to meet his eyes, and then turned away to say something to Peter. What was going on? Nathan said he liked spending time with her. Why wouldn't he be happy about her staying for longer?

* * *

There was time for a bit more of a kick around in the garden before Andrew and his family needed to head home to get the children to bed. There was no opportunity for Jessica to get Nathan alone and talk to him, but she was determined to before the evening was over.

Jessica went to the front door to say goodbye to her nieces and nephew.

"Can I really come to ballet with you, Aunt Jessica?" asked Emily as she gave Jessica a hug goodbye.

"Yes, of course. The class for you and Sophie is on Saturday morning at ten o'clock if you'd like to come."

"I want to come!" piped up Sophie. "I can already do twirls," she added, demonstrating her talent and nearly sending her older sister flying.

"That's brilliant," Jessica said. "I can pick them up and drop them back home if you like?" she said to Molly.

"Would you be happy with that, girls?" Molly asked.

"Yes!" the girls chorused.

"There's a class for older kids that you could try out if you like, Peter," Jessica offered.

The panic on her nephew's face immediately told Jessica that ballet really wasn't his thing.

"It's OK if you'd rather not," she said quickly.

Relief washed over him and he said, "I think I prefer football to dancing."

"That's cool. I'm sorry I can't play football with you at the moment, but maybe I could take you all to the cinema soon?"

"Can we go and see the new Sonic film?" Peter asked. "It looks awesome."

"Sure. Would you like to see that one too, girls?"

"Yes, please," said Emily. Sophie nodded.

"Great. I'll sort that out with your parents then."

Jessica went back into the kitchen where her mum was clearing up.

"Can I give you a hand with that?" she asked.

"Not if it will hurt your foot," Sarah said firmly.

"I can load the dishwasher if you pile the dirty stuff on the side for me," Jessica suggested.

"All right, thank you, but stop if it's making your foot ache."

"I will, I promise. Are Dad and Nathan still outside?"

"Yeah, they're getting along well. Nathan was saying that he took you canoeing on Saturday, and your dad wanted to show him that old paddle that he's had for years in the shed."

"I remember that thing. Didn't we use it with an inflatable dinghy once?"

"Yes, in the pond near your grandma's house," Sarah said, laughing.

They continued working in silence until the dishwasher was on and anything that wouldn't fit in it was stacked up on the side.

"Nathan's lovely," Sarah said, filling up the kettle.

"He is," agreed Jessica.

"I'm guessing he's single as you were staying with him."

"Yes. He's just divorced, actually."

"Oh no, what a shame." Jessica couldn't help noticing that her mother didn't look like it was much of a shame that Nathan was back on the market. "Do you know what happened?"

"No, only that that's why he moved back here."

Joe walked in from the garden followed by Nathan.

"Oh, you needn't have done that, love," Joe said, putting his arm around his wife. "I would have helped."

"Jessica gave me a hand so it was no trouble. Would you like a tea or coffee, Nathan?"

"No, thank you," he said. "I'd better be getting home. I've left my dog by himself."

"Oh, you should have brought him with you!" Joe declared. "Does he get on well with Monty?"

"Yes, they're great friends."

"We'll have to get them together for some walks," Joe said.

"Dennis would like that. Thank you. And thank you for a lovely evening."

"It was our pleasure," said Sarah.

"I'll come out with you," Jessica said. There was no way he was getting away without talking to her.

She waited until they were outside the front door. She pulled it closed behind them so they were definitely out of her parents' earshot before she said, "You didn't seem very happy about me staying for longer."

"What? Of course I am. I've been worrying about you going back to your apartment and struggling with the stairs . . ."

Jessica glared at him. "I saw your face when I made my announcement."

Nathan sighed. "I was surprised."

"I thought it would be a good surprise," Jessica said quietly. She was trying not to get upset, but she really couldn't understand Nathan's reaction. She'd been so excited when she'd made her decision; why wouldn't he want her to hang around?

"It was," he said. "A good surprise. It's just . . . I'd prepared myself for you leaving."

"And you're sorry I'm not?"

"No! Not at all. Jess." He reached out to hold her hand. Jessica didn't remove hers and tried to ignore her body's reaction to it as goosebumps travelled up her arm. "I don't imagine I've been able to hide how much I like you. I think you're amazing, and it's been so great having you here. But I think I was able to hold it together around you because I knew you were only going to be here for a short amount of time. And now you're going to stay for longer . . . let's just say I think I'm going to struggle." He gave her an embarrassed smile.

"Oh." Jessica swallowed hard. She had really not expected that.

"Sorry if I've made things awkward . . ."

"No, you haven't," she said quickly. "Thank you for telling me. I think you're pretty amazing too, you know, and if it wasn't for . . . well a lot of stuff . . ."

"A whole lot of stuff . . ."

"Yeah . . . If you'd rather we didn't . . . hang out . . ."

"No, I want to . . . hang out with you," he said, his eyes meeting hers, making her smile.

"Good."

"I'm sorry I was weird."

"That's OK, I get it," said Jessica. She gave him as good a hug as she could manage with crutches.

"*Fable* night soon?"

"I'm free tomorrow."

"See you around six then?"

"Perfect," Jessica said. She kissed his cheek. "I'll see you then."

Jessica watched Nathan walk down the street. Would it be more sensible for them to stay apart? Maybe, but she really didn't want to. She loved spending time with Nathan, and yes, she had a crush on him, but that would pass. It would be stupid to give up their friendship just because every time she looked at his mouth she wasn't able to prevent herself from thinking about what it would be like to kiss it again.

* * *

Jessica was nervous as she stood outside Nathan's house the following evening. Her muscles ached as she lifted her arm to ring the doorbell. She was pleased. She'd worked out a lot today as well as taking care of all the admin involved with her staying for longer, and it was good that her body was feeling it. It was nice to be physically tired from exercise again, even if she couldn't do everything she'd like to.

Nathan opened the door. "I forgot you'd need to ring the bell now," he said. "Come on in." He stepped aside to let Jessica pass.

Dennis stood by his master, his tail wagging crazily.

"Hello, boy." Jessica gave him a pat. "Have you missed me?"

"You and Monty," said Nathan. "He's been by himself all day."

"Poor little guy." Jessica followed Nathan into the kitchen. "Maybe I could pop in to see him sometimes while I'm still here? Keep him company for an hour or so."

"He'd love that."

"It's a shame I couldn't bring Monty to visit, but I couldn't manage to get him here on my crutches."

"No, that would be a recipe for disaster," Nathan agreed. "You will stay for dinner, won't you?"

"Yes, please. Do I have to help cook, though?"

"It'll get it done faster."

"Hand me a chopping board."

* * *

They sat down to home-made chilli con carne and fluffy white rice an hour later.

128

"This is so good," Jessica said, putting another forkful into her mouth.

"I'm not sure I should have let you be in charge of adding the chilli powder," Nathan said before gulping down more water. Jessica watched his lips parting as the glass met them again, and his Adam's apple bob as he swallowed. A shiver of desire passed through her.

"When are you next helping out at the dance studio?" Nathan asked, bringing her attention back to the conversation.

"Tomorrow. It's the older students so it should be really interesting. Diana also wants to go over some of the lesson plans with me so that I know what each student is aiming towards."

"It's great that she's paying you."

"I know. That money combined with the insurance payout from my company will mean that this month is probably the most I've ever earned as a dancer."

"I take it dancers don't get paid very well?"

"It's not terrible," said Jessica. "And I would have got a raise when I started rehearsals for *The Sleeping Beauty* because of moving up to being a principal dancer, but people certainly don't go into it for the money."

"I guess you really have to love it to want to do it for a career."

"Yeah, I can't imagine doing anything else."

Nathan looked down at his plate and was silent for a moment before he said, "You'll need to at some point, though."

"You mean in case my foot doesn't heal properly?" Jessica wished Nathan wasn't bringing up her injury now. They'd been having such a nice evening.

"Yes, and also because of your age," Nathan said carefully.

"What about my age?" Jessica put her fork down.

Nathan looked like he wished he could be transported as far away as possible. "Forget I said anything. It doesn't matter."

"I'm guessing that you mean that because I'm thirty-one, I'll soon be over the hill?"

"I wouldn't have put it quite like that, but you must know you're reaching the end of your ballet career. I looked it up and most dancers end their careers around age thirty-five."

"And some continue for a lot longer," Jessica said coldly. She took a sip of her drink and took a deep breath. "Do you like being a doctor?"

"I love being a doctor, most of the time," replied Nathan.

"Did you ever think you might become something else?"

"Sure, I wanted to be a firefighter for a while when I was small, and then an astronaut."

"You see," explained Jessica, "I've only ever wanted to be a dancer. The only thing I can remember ever having any interest in being was a ballerina. There simply wasn't an option for me to be anything else. Ballet is so much a part of me. I don't know what I'd be without ballet."

"Can I be honest with you?" asked Nathan.

"Of course," Jessica said automatically, although she really wasn't sure she was going to like what he had to say.

"I think your foot is going to be completely fine in just a few weeks. You'll need to be careful for a while and build the strength back up in it gradually, but there's no reason why you can't dance again professionally."

Jessica gave him a small smile of thanks.

"However," he continued gently, "you know as well as I do that you won't be able to dance professionally for ever. Every ballet dancer's career has a shelf life. You need to be planning ahead and thinking about what you're going to do when your dancing career comes to an end."

"I've got plenty of time to think about that. I've got years of dancing ahead of me!" retorted Jessica, seeing red. "I'd only just been made a principal ballerina before my foot was injured. I'm at the top of my career."

"Yes, but at some point the descent begins, and if the past couple of weeks has taught you anything it should be that that descent could happen at any time. You need to have a backup plan."

Jessica's stomach dropped and she felt sick as all the insecurities and worries she'd carried around for so long flashed into her mind en masse.

"Backup plans just divide your attention and shorten your career faster. You have to give it everything. But I don't know why I'm explaining myself! I really don't think it's your place to tell me what to do with my life!" she said, an edge to her voice as she struggled to control her temper. She failed. "It's none of your business whether I have a plan for when I retire from ballet, however many years in the future that might be. It's not like you're doing such a great job with your own life. You're divorced and living in a house that's like a show home, throwing out life advice like you're some kind of expert! Maybe if you had more of a life yourself, you wouldn't feel such a need to interfere in everyone else's. No wonder your wife left you. She probably had passion and drive for something you didn't approve of and got fed up with you trying to stamp it out of her!"

Jessica regretted her words as soon as they were out of her mouth. The look on Nathan's face made her say immediately, "Nathan . . ."

"I think it would be best if you left," he said quietly.

"I think so too. I can see myself out." Jessica picked up her crutches and her bag and walked out of the house without looking back.

CHAPTER ELEVEN

Jessica was still fuming when she walked to the dance studio the following afternoon. How dare Nathan think he had the right to tell her what to do with her life! Just because he had no passion for anything didn't mean that everyone should be like that. And it was none of his business what she did with her life anyway.

It was calming to be in the dance studio, though, seeing the teenagers go through the familiar routines. She watched each of them carefully, noting their strengths as well as their weaknesses.

The class finished and the dancers left, leaving just Diana and Jessica.

"Let's go into my office and we can work our way through the students so you've got a better idea of what they're aiming towards," Diana said.

Jessica followed Diana into the little office. The last time she'd been in there was when she'd told Diana that she'd been accepted into the ballet school in London. Diana had spent months helping Jessica to prepare for her audition and had been absolutely thrilled to hear her star pupil's news.

Jessica accepted the seat offered and looked around the room. It hadn't changed very much since she was last there.

She smiled when she spotted a poster of a performance she'd been in of *The Nutcracker* on the wall. She'd been in the corps when she'd performed in it.

Diana followed her gaze. "Your mother and father were so proud of you when they saw your performance in that. They brought me back the poster as a souvenir."

Jessica wasn't sure she remembered her mum and dad coming to see that ballet. She was always so busy before and after a performance, there was little time to speak to anyone who'd come to watch, especially because she would have been sharing a busy, crowded dressing room at the time.

"So, what did you think of the dancers today?" Diana asked.

"I'm afraid I couldn't see any that had any real potential," Jessica said, honestly. She felt bad for saying so because she thought Diana did a wonderful job, but she didn't want to lie. "The girl at the back, I think her name was Poppy, had good arms, and there was a boy, Jason, who showed some promise."

Diana smiled. "A very fair assessment," she agreed. "I don't believe I have any students at the moment who will take up ballet professionally."

"But", said Jessica, "what's the point of the dance school if there isn't a single student attending who has any real talent?"

"Oh Jessica," said Diana kindly, "have you got any idea how unusual it is for a dance school of this size, located in a little town, to produce a world-class ballerina? I struck extremely lucky when I taught you, but I doubt I'll be that lucky again."

"You've been training dancers for more than twenty-five years, and you've only had one turn professional? Isn't that kind of . . . disappointing?"

"I don't think so," Diana said carefully. She was silent for a moment and then continued, "For some, ballet becomes a profession, for others it can be something they enjoy, a way to keep fit, or something to give them confidence or make them feel beautiful. These are all valid reasons for coming to my class, and those dancers are just as important as the ones who show more promise and might want to dance professionally.

Take that boy Jason that you mentioned. When he first came here, he was being bullied for being scrawny. He wanted to become stronger but didn't have any interest in the team sports his school ran. He started dancing and now he lifts weights as well. His confidence has soared and a couple of other boys from his year have joined as well. I don't teach to produce ballerinas — I teach to pass on my love of ballet."

"I guess I've never seen it like that before," admitted Jessica. "How did you know teaching was for you?"

"Honestly, I didn't. I took a chance when I was offered a job, and then set up this school when I discovered I was good at teaching and loved doing it."

The horrible conversation with Nathan still fresh in her mind, Jessica asked, "Do you mind me asking how old you were when you retired from dancing professionally?"

"Not at all — I was twenty-seven."

"So young. Were you injured?" Jessica found herself asking. But did she really want to hear the answer? What if Diana admitted she'd broken her foot and that's what had ended her dancing career?

"I got fed up," she said simply.

"Fed up with dancing?"

"No, I still loved dancing, but I was worried that if I carried on, it wouldn't be long before I did fall out of love with it. I was fed up with my muscles always aching, of having to watch everything I ate, of always having to go to bed early. I was never as talented as you. I knew deep down I was never going to be a principal, but I worried that if I spent ten more years trying, I'd miss out on so many other things."

"And so you think you made the right decision?" asked Jessica.

"Yes," replied Diana, thoughtfully. "I've got some wonderful memories of that life, but it was the right time to leave." She was silent for a moment before asking, "Why all the questions? Are you thinking about quitting?"

"No," Jessica said immediately. "Nathan and I — the guy I was staying with — had an argument last night and it's got me thinking."

"An argument about what?"

"He thinks I'm getting old." Jessica grimaced.

"He said that?" Diana's eyes were wide.

"Well, not exactly," Jessica admitted. "He pointed out that I may not have many years left of my ballet career, even if my foot does heal properly. He thinks I need a plan for afterwards."

Diana smiled. "That's not quite the same as saying you're getting old, but I don't imagine it was very nice to hear! I'm guessing you haven't got a post-dance career planned?"

"Not really . . . I mean, my company has stuff set up to help dancers to retrain and find employment after they retire, but I haven't looked into it much. All I've ever wanted is to be a professional ballerina."

"Unfortunately, no ballet dancer can carry on professionally indefinitely," said Diana. "And it's hard for people outside of the ballet world to grasp how much it means and how hard it is to make the decision to stop."

Jessica nodded.

"It sounds like your friend's a practical person and is trying to look out for you, just not going about it the right way."

"I guess. I didn't take it very well."

"It's not an easy thing to come to terms with. But it's a fact of life. You've achieved so much in your career, and I'm sure you'll achieve plenty more, but at some point, it will end, unfortunately, earlier than the majority of jobs."

"I just don't know what else I could possibly want to do," admitted Jessica. "I like helping you teach, but I'm really not sure it's for me long-term, and what else can I do?"

"I think that's a problem a lot of dancers have," said Diana. "They give so much to their dance career that when it ends they're not necessarily trained for anything else. But you've got plenty of time to work out what you'd like to do. You've got years of dancing still in you."

"Thanks, Diana."

"No problem. And don't be too hard on Nathan. No one outside the ballet world truly understands what it's like and how much of yourself you give to it. I believe he was trying to be practical rather than unkind."

"I think you're right," Jessica said. "I'm sorry, but do you mind if I head off? There's someone I really need to speak to."

"Of course not, I'll see you tomorrow," said Diana kindly.

* * *

Jessica hurried out of the dance studio, almost forgetting her bag in her haste. She had to speak to Nathan. She still thought he could have worded his concerns better, but Diana was right; he was looking out for her. He didn't understand what it was like to feel the way she did about ballet, but that didn't mean he was being unkind. She was grateful he cared about her enough to think about these things. And she never should have said the things she'd said to him. She'd been angry and had spoken without thinking. She didn't know what had happened in his marriage, but she did know that Nathan was kind, loving and trustworthy. It had been horrible to say he'd driven his wife away. And of course she hadn't meant it.

She considered taking a detour and stopping off at the supermarket to pick something up by way of apology, but she wanted to get to Nathan's as soon as possible. Maybe she could treat them to a takeaway? She'd need to text her mum and let her know she wouldn't be home for supper.

Jessica turned the corner into Nathan's road and immediately noticed that his Land Rover wasn't parked outside his house. She checked her watch; he should be back from work now. Maybe he'd taken Dennis out for a walk further afield? Should she wait? She could message him, but it didn't feel right to apologise that way. She needed to do it face to face. Sadly, she turned around and began walking back to her parents' house, her heart heavy, wishing she'd been able to make things right.

* * *

Jessica was restless for the whole of the following day. She wanted to see Nathan and do her best to make things right with him. It wasn't only that she felt terrible about what had happened, which she really did, but she was also missing spending time with him. She continually checked her phone to see if he'd messaged. He didn't seem the sort to hold a grudge, and they usually messaged each other regularly . . . She'd really hurt him.

She wanted to go and see him before going to the ballet studios, but there was little point as he wouldn't be home from work yet anyway. She made herself hang on until after-wards, but was disappointed to see his Land Rover still missing from the driveway. She rang the doorbell, just in case, but there was no reply.

* * *

There weren't any classes at the dance studio on Thursday, so Jessica had even more time on her hands. Time to worry about where Nathan was, and whether he'd be willing to forgive her when she finally got around to seeing him. Once more she stared at her phone, willing it to ding with a message from him, and debating whether she should send one herself.

Her mum was out helping her dad at the estate agent's for the afternoon and Jessica needed something to keep busy. In the back of her mind was what Diana and Nathan had both said about her needing to come up with a plan for when she finished dancing. She was still determined to be dancing for many years to come — she had a long bucket list of roles she wanted to dance — but she had to admit it made sense to be prepared. She also knew she needed something else in her life when she returned to New York. It would take months to build up the strength in her foot again, and she needed something to take her mind off her convalescence when she didn't even have helping Diana with her classes to keep her occupied.

137

The obvious job was for her to teach, but the more she thought about it, the more Jessica realised it wasn't a good fit. She thought what Diana did was wonderful, and she saw what a difference Diana's classes could make to the children and adults who attended them, and she was enjoying helping out, but doing it full-time wouldn't be right for her, she felt. Neither would training professional dancers in a company. The politics involved behind the scenes of a ballet company were not something she'd ever want to be involved in. There was also the fact that she might not be able to if injury was what led to the end of her career.

She sat down with a cup of coffee, taking the opportunity to rest her foot before venturing around to Nathan's house again later. She picked up her iPad and began scrolling through her favourite ballet Substack blogs. She was sort of glad that nobody from her own company ran one. Rehearsals would have started on Monday, and she wasn't sure she was ready to see the photos. She remembered how much she'd loved reading about professional dancers when she was a teenager. She'd spend hours poring over entries detailing their daily lives and the exercises and practices they did. It had been amazing for her that she'd been able to read about dancers from all around the world, and seeing the photos and descriptions of them performing had encouraged her to keep going and to follow her dream, even when things got tough.

When it got to the point that Nathan should be home from work, Jessica got up and checked herself in the hallway mirror. Monty gave her a really pathetic 'Will you take me with you?' look.

"I'm sorry, Monty. I can't," she said. "But your dad will be home soon."

Monty's head fell.

"You really know how to make me feel bad, don't you? I promise I'll play ball with you in the garden when I get back," she said as she went out the front door.

* * *

She walked as quickly as she could manage on her crutches to Nathan's house and was thrilled to see his car parked outside. She rang the doorbell, steeling herself. She reminded herself that he might not forgive her right away, but she had to try her best. She waited but Nathan didn't answer the door. She rang the doorbell a second time, but still nothing.

Feeling completely deflated, she walked back to her parents' home again.

* * *

On Friday, Jessica decided to do herself a favour and not check Nathan's house after she finished helping at the two dance classes held that evening. It was late and she was hungry, and she felt like she was going crazy trying to catch Nathan when she suspected he didn't want to be caught. She wished she was spending the evening hanging out with him, but there wasn't anything she could do about that now. She'd go back to her parents' house, heat up some leftovers for supper, and veg in front of the television for a while to give her foot a rest. Maybe she'd even work out what she could say in a WhatsApp message to open communications between them again, as it looked like that was the best option.

Her mum and dad were both home and Andrew was with them in the kitchen.

"Hey, sis," he said.

"Hi, Andrew, where are Molly and the kids?"

"At home. I just popped by to borrow Dad's strimmer. Are you still OK to take the girls to ballet tomorrow?"

"Yeah, sure," Jessica said, distractedly as she looked in the fridge for something to eat.

"What's up with you, sweetheart?" asked Sarah, noticing her daughter's peculiar mood.

"I'm all right. Just a bit tired."

"Is your foot hurting you?"

"A little," she admitted. "I'll prop it up on the sofa in a bit."

"Are you sure there's nothing else?"

Jessica closed the fridge door. "Actually, there is. Nathan and I had a big fight on Monday. It was really stupid and I overreacted completely to what he was saying, and I feel really bad about it." She hadn't expected to share this but was immediately glad that she had.

"I was wondering why he hadn't been around and why you weren't spending time with him over the past few days," said Joe.

"I really want to apologise, but I think he's avoiding me. I've been to his house several times and he's not answering the door, even when his car's in the driveway," Jessica explained.

"I saw him yesterday," Andrew offered.

"You did? Where?" Jessica said, leaping on this information. "Is he all right?"

"He seemed fine." Andrew shrugged. "He's joined my five-a-side team and he came to training. He's a lot fitter than the rest of us."

"Did he mention me at all?" Jessica braved asking.

"Nope," admitted Andrew, "but we were blokes playing football . . . none of us really talk about our wives or girlfriends."

"I'm not his girlfriend," Jessica said quickly. She saw a look pass between her mum and dad before she said, "Do you know if he's home tonight?"

"I do, actually. I messaged him earlier to see if he fancied a pint. He said he was going to be spending the evening at home with his dog."

"Thanks, Andrew!" called Jessica over her shoulder as she headed out of the house again. She *would* catch Nathan.

It had started to drizzle, and she wished she'd thought to bring a jacket with her, but no way was she going to turn back. Thankfully she was pretty fast on her crutches now.

Nathan's Land Rover was there. She walked up to the front door and rang the bell. Her heart sank when no one answered. Despondent, she turned to leave, but the door opened and there was Nathan with Dennis by his side. He gave her a little smile. "Hey you," he said, softly.

Momentarily flummoxed, Jessica forgot what she was going to say. If anything, he was even more handsome and he somehow, magically, hadn't just slammed the door in her face.

"Hi," she said finally.

"Would you like to come in?" he asked.

"Yes, please," she said. Nathan moved aside so she could get past him, but Jessica stayed where she was.

"I'm so sorry," she blurted out. "I never should have said those terrible things, and I regret them so much."

"Come inside, I'll get us a drink."

Jessica nodded and followed him into the house.

"I've been trying to catch you for the last few evenings, but you haven't been in," she explained.

"I've been out. Trying to get a life," Nathan said with a wry smile.

Jessica sat down at the kitchen table and put her head in her hands. "I can't believe the things I said."

"You were pretty harsh," admitted Nathan, handing her a beer.

"I was upset . . ." she began.

"I know," interrupted Nathan. "And I'm sorry too. You're right — it's none of my business and I was interfering. It's your decision whatever you decide to do when you finish dancing, and you don't have to explain yourself to me. It's just that I care about you."

"I know you do, and I should have reacted better. Can we put it behind us and go back to being friends, do you think?" she asked.

"I'd like that," Nathan said. Jessica stood up and she moved into his open arms and they hugged.

"I've missed you," she said as they broke apart. "Where have you been, really?"

"I was quite serious." Nathan laughed. "I've been getting a life. I've lived here for a few months now, but I haven't made much of an effort to make friends so I'm trying to remedy that. I've been out for a meal with some people from work, and I visited my sister, and I played football with your brother and his mates last night."

"He told me. That's how I knew you'd be home now," admitted Jessica.

"I used the excuse of not wanting to leave Dennis by himself again, but, honestly, I needed a night off myself from all the socialising." Nathan grimaced.

"Your little experiment hasn't been a success, then?"

"It kind of has. I've had a good time, but honestly, I would much rather have been spending my evenings with you."

"Well, I haven't had a good time at all," admitted Jessica. "I've been miserable without you to hang out with."

"Why didn't you call or message?"

"I wanted to apologise to your face," she said. "Why didn't you get in touch with me?"

"To begin with, I was too angry," Nathan explained. "Then, once I'd calmed down, I realised there was some truth in what you said about me not having much of a life, and I wanted to prove to you that I could remedy that."

"I was stupid to say that. I only did it because I was mad. And I'm hardly one to talk about work–life balance. You should never listen to anything I say."

"I'll try to bear that in mind," Nathan said with a smile.

"And what I said about you and your wife . . ." She still couldn't believe she'd done that. "You're so lovely. I don't actually believe you did anything to make Claire leave you. She's obviously a complete weirdo."

"Thank you, but she's really not," Nathan said. "We broke up because it turns out we wanted very different things."

"You don't have to tell me any of this . . ."

"It's OK. I want to." He ran his fingers through his hair before he continued. "She's a doctor as well. We met at medical school. We got together in our final year. Anyway, my wanting to be a GP was always a bit of a bone of contention

142

between us. She tried to convince me to be a surgeon and to join a private clinic, but that just wasn't me."

Jessica nodded; she definitely couldn't imagine Nathan as a private surgeon.

"Then Claire decided she didn't want to practise medicine. She took a job with a pharmaceutical company. It paid really well, and she travelled the world with them, which she loved. I was honestly really happy for her, but it got to the point where she was travelling so much we hardly saw each other. We should have talked about it earlier, but I knew how much she loved her job, and I didn't want to spoil that for her. It all came to a head when she was offered a position in Tokyo for six months. I said I didn't want us to be apart for that long. She wanted to go, so she did."

"I'm so sorry."

Nathan nodded sadly. "It was really hard at the time. When she came back, we tried to make it work, but we were two people who just occasionally lived together at that point. When she got offered another placement, this time in Berlin, we called it quits."

"That sucks."

"Thanks," said Nathan with a sigh. "In hindsight, we never should have got married. We both wanted completely different things in life. She was far more driven than me, and I was proud of her, but there wasn't space for me as well as her career."

"You deserve better than that," Jessica said.

"Thank you. Anyway, that's the sad tale of my failed marriage."

"I'm glad you told me."

"I'm glad too."

Jessica's stomach growled noisily. "Sorry!" she said with a laugh.

"You're hungry?" Nathan asked.

"A bit. I was helping Diana and then I was going to eat at Mum and Dad's but I heard you were home so I hurried straight over."

"Do you want to hang out here for a while?" offered Nathan. "I cooked way too much for supper — I can heat you up some if you like . . . and we could play a bit of *Fable II*?"

Jessica grinned. "That sounds absolutely brilliant."

* * *

Jessica set off on her crutches to pick up Emily and Sophie for their first ballet class the following morning. She felt so much lighter now she and Nathan were back on an even keel. She wasn't used to relying on a friend as much as she did him, and it had been completely discombobulating not to have him around.

Andrew opened the door to his family's cute three-bedroom cottage on the edge of the town when she knocked.

"Hey, sis," he said, gesturing to her to come in. "Fancy a quick coffee?"

Jessica checked her watch. "Thank you, that would be great."

She followed her brother into the kitchen at the back of the house where Molly was clearing up after breakfast.

"Hiya. Did you manage to get everything sorted out with Nathan last night?" Molly asked. "Andrew said you two had argued."

"Yes, thanks," said Jessica, blushing. "Where are the kids?" She needed to change the subject.

"Playing in the garden. I'll call the girls in to get changed," Molly said.

"I'll do it," offered Andrew, "if you get the coffee machine on."

"Deal," said Molly.

Jessica found it interesting to watch her brother and his wife together. She didn't know Molly very well. She'd never had the opportunity to spend much time with her sister-in-law, but she and Andrew seemed to work well together. They were comfortable with one another and just seemed to fit.

Molly handed Jessica her coffee at the same time as Jessica's nieces and nephew came crashing in from the garden, closely followed by their father. All three of the children were still in pyjamas and were distinctly mud-covered.

"Oh no! What have you guys been doing out there?" gasped Molly. "You girls need to leave for your class in a few minutes!"

"We were just playing . . ." explained Emily.

"Let's get you upstairs and I'll give you a hand getting clean and ready," Molly said with a sigh. "Sorry, Jessica," she called over her shoulder. "I'll have them sorted in just a few minutes."

"No worries." Jessica laughed as Molly shooed the children up the stairs. Her nieces definitely didn't look like they would be in a ballet studio soon.

"The girls have really been looking forward to this class," Andrew said. "They made Molly buy them leotards especially."

"That's good. I hope they enjoy it."

"So do I. But I have to admit, I'm praying they don't enjoy it too much."

"You don't want them to turn into ballet-crazed lunatics like their aunt?" Jessica guessed.

"Something like that . . ."

"I understand it can be a bit of a pain for the rest of the family."

"Just a bit," admitted Andrew.

"I'm sorry. I don't think I ever really considered how hard it must have been at times for you."

"You were a kid."

"Still . . ."

"I don't blame you," he said. "It wasn't your fault you had this ridiculously amazing talent. And I had a great childhood. It's just not what I'd want for my family."

"I understand," said Jessica. "I'll keep my fingers crossed for you that they both have two left feet."

"I'd appreciate that."

* * *

145

"Please say you haven't got any plans for next Saturday night?" said Nathan when Jessica answered the phone to him the following morning.

"I don't have any plans for next Saturday night," she said. "Are we doing something fun?"

"I wanted to celebrate us being friends again, so I've got us tickets to see *Swan Lake* at the Sadler's Wells Theatre."

"That's so lovely of you, but you don't have to sit through ballet for me," Jessica said immediately.

"I want to. I've never been to the ballet before, and it's important to you. It'll be a new life experience, which I get to do with someone who knows all about it and can fill me in on anything I don't understand."

"Are you sure you wouldn't rather do something else?"

"Nope."

"In that case, that sounds absolutely brilliant!" said Jessica excitedly. "It's the Bolshoi Ballet, isn't it?"

"It is indeed. How did you know that?"

"Ballet crazy, remember? Can I go halves on the tickets?"

"You may not," Nathan said, firmly.

"In that case, I'm treating you to supper first."

"That sounds great."

* * *

Jessica didn't get back to her parents' house until four in the afternoon the following Saturday after working at the dance studio, which didn't give her much time to get ready. Nathan was picking her up in half an hour. He'd wanted to drive them into London so she wouldn't have to walk, but she pointed out that if the traffic was bad, which it invariably would be, then it would take far longer than going by train and the underground to Angel. In the end, Nathan wouldn't budge though and Jessica had given in. Thinking about trying to traverse the London underground with crutches, she was glad that Nathan had stuck to his guns.

She was pleased that she'd packed a couple of nice dresses in case she ended up going out somewhere in the evening. She redid her make-up and curled her hair, though it was so thick the curls probably wouldn't stay in it for long. She pulled on the black cocktail dress she'd chosen, lamenting the fact that, because of her foot, she couldn't wear shoes that would go with it and was stuck in trainers.

Nathan was on time, as she'd known he would be. She'd never had a friend as reliable as he was.

He'd downloaded a recording of Tchaikovsky's score, which they played in the car with Jessica explaining the story to him.

"That's pretty tragic," commented Nathan.

"Yep!"

They parked on a side street.

"Where would you like to eat?" Nathan asked. "We haven't got long."

"Banana Tree," said Jessica automatically. "They're quick and the food is yummy. I discovered it when I was dancing here a few years ago."

"You've danced at Sadler's Wells?" asked Nathan, his eyebrows raised.

"I was in *The Nutcracker* here one Christmas. It was an amazing experience."

* * *

They walked to the restaurant and sat down opposite each other on the benches running along the long wooden tables. They ordered sparkling waters and Jessica chose the Singapore laksa with grilled chicken, while Nathan opted for pad thai.

"This is really good," Nathan said, tucking into his meal.

"Told ya," said Jessica, smiling. "I came here practically every day for lunch during that run of *The Nutcracker*. Oh, before I forget, my mum and dad were wondering if you're free to come to dinner tomorrow. Dennis is invited too."

Nathan smiled at her. "Sure, I'd love to." He held her gaze for a moment before going back to his pad thai.

They finished, Jessica paid, and the pair walked to the theatre together. "I should have said before, you look really beautiful this evening," said Nathan.

"Even with my trainers? Or should I say, trainer."

"Even with your trainer," confirmed Nathan.

They entered the theatre. Jessica felt Nathan's warm hand on the small of her back as they moved between the crowds and into the auditorium.

"Good seats," commented Jessica as they sat down.

"I googled to find out which ones had the most legroom and the best view," admitted Nathan.

"Thank you." Jessica was so touched.

"Would you like a programme?"

"Absolutely — I've kept every programme from every ballet performance I've ever attended."

"I'll go and get you one," Nathan said. "I'm worried about your foot getting knocked with it being so busy out there."

"Thanks."

He left and Jessica took the opportunity to look around, taking in her surroundings and working out what she felt about being back in this world again, even if it was in front of the stage rather than behind. She could imagine exactly what was happening on the other side of the dusty velvet curtains. Everyone hurrying around, warming up, stage hands getting props in place. Nerves would be on edge. She smiled as she recalled the many times she'd stood in the wings, feeling sick with anticipation, going through the sequences in her head, doing her best to block out the busyness around her. She couldn't imagine never doing that again.

* * *

Nathan watched Jessica as he made his way back to his seat with her programme in his hand. She looked beautiful. What was she thinking? She seemed pleased to be here, though he'd doubted the wisdom of bringing her almost as soon as he'd purchased the tickets. Would she be upset seeing the dancers on stage doing what she was currently unable to? By that point, though, there was no turning back. Turned out decent tickets to see a ballet were pretty pricey.

But they were having a really nice evening and he was glad he was getting to experience going to the ballet with Jessica. It was such a huge part of her life, he wanted to understand more and be at least a tiny bit involved in it.

The lights went down and anticipation filled the air as the curtains opened to reveal the beginning of the ballet. Nathan glanced across at Jessica. She was on the edge of her seat, totally enthralled, already enchanted by the performance.

* * *

The curtains closed for the interval and only then did Jessica sit back in her seat.

"What did you think?" asked Nathan, smiling. It was obvious that she was having a wonderful time.

"Brilliant!" Jessica replied. "Absolutely magical. What about you?"

"I'm glad you talked me through the story earlier, but I'm still a bit confused," he admitted. "I'm enjoying it more than I thought I would, though."

"Good," said Jessica happily.

"Do you want to stay here for the break?"

"No, can we go for a bit of a walk around? I need to move."

"Sure. Let me go first, though, so I can clear the way."

"Like I'm a queen?"

"Absolutely."

* * *

When they returned to their seats and the ballet started up again, Jessica stayed sitting back in her seat and leaned in close to Nathan, whispering to him about what was going

149

on. She smelled of something light and floral, and her hair tickled his cheek occasionally.

"Thank you," he whispered back, taking her hand without thinking about it.

He'd definitely never had a friendship that made him feel like this, but as much as Nathan told himself that he needed to protect himself and hold himself back from giving too much to Jessica, it seems he was determined not to listen. She squeezed his hand gently to signal what a lovely time she was having, and Nathan had to conclude, he was a goner.

* * *

They came out of the theatre into night-time London.

"That was brilliant." Jessica looked up at Nathan with shining eyes. "Thank you so much. Did you like it?"

"It was my pleasure. I did like it, the company in particular," he said. He frowned. "Are you cold?"

"A little," admitted Jessica.

Nathan took off his jacket and helped her on with it.

"Now you'll be cold," she pointed out.

"I'm fine," he said with a grin. "Us men are made of stern stuff."

Jessica laughed. "Sure you are. Shall we head back to the car?"

"If you'd like. I know of an ice-cream parlour around here, though, that's supposed to be really good. It's open until ten."

"That sounds great!" she said. "I'm still too excited to go home."

"And you think sugar's going to help with that?"

She laughed again. "Definitely."

They walked along together, Jessica filling Nathan in about when she lived in London while she was at ballet school. "I was so busy that I never really had a lot of time to sightsee. But I did get taken out to some amazing places by my company for fundraisers," she said.

They reached the ice-cream parlour, which had a steady stream of customers, mostly theatregoers like themselves.

Nathan had a honey and honeycomb ice cream and Jessica a pear sorbet. They got them in tubs to take away but soon realised that Jessica wasn't able to walk on crutches and eat her sorbet at the same time, so they stopped at a bench and sat down.

"This is amazing," said Jessica. "Do you want to try some?"

"Sure," said Nathan, and they swapped pots.

"How did you even know about this ice-cream parlour?"

"I looked it up," he said.

"You've planned a perfect evening."

"That was the idea." Nathan was blushing.

"Well, you succeeded."

"A perfect evening with a perfect woman." Nathan swapped pots back again.

"I'm far from perfect," said Jessica. She shook her head. "Especially after what I said to you when we had that argument . . ."

"Hey," Nathan said kindly, turning her to face him. "I thought we'd agreed that was all water under the bridge? We've both apologised."

"I know, but that doesn't mean I don't still feel bad about it," Jessica said, hanging her head.

"Me too," Nathan admitted. "I never should have tried to tell you what to do. But it's over, and we're friends again now."

He put his arm around her and she looked up at him. "You've got ice cream on your face," she said, smiling affectionately. She reached up and gently wiped it off.

She stopped, her eyes meeting his. It felt like the most natural thing in the world for her to then lean in and kiss him.

The world stopped as their lips met, sparks flying through Jessica's whole body as they tentatively gave in to what their bodies craved.

"Wow," Nathan said when they pulled apart.

"You taste of honey," said Jessica, grinning.

"That was . . ."

"Amazing," finished Jessica.

"We can't blame beer this time," Nathan said.

"I didn't honestly blame the beer last time."

"Me neither. Can I kiss you again?" Nathan asked. "I'm beginning to doubt it was as good as I thought it was. It can't possibly have been."

"It probably would be a good idea to check," agreed Jessica.

This time it was Nathan who leaned in and the kiss was longer. He put an arm around her waist, coaxing her towards him.

"Well, this is a new, fun side to our friendship," said Jessica when they finally came up for air.

"It certainly is." Nathan ran his fingers through her hair. "But . . ."

Jessica pressed a finger to his lips. "No, buts," she said, gently. "Maybe this isn't the best idea, but, honestly, I'm fed up with pretending I don't want to do this with you."

She held her breath, waiting to see how Nathan would respond. Would he let her down gently? He'd been through so much with his ex-wife, was it even fair of her to push him into this whatever it was, which had no future to it?

"I really like you," Nathan said.

"I really like you too. And we're both consenting adults. Maybe this is just a lust thing, maybe if we just get it out of our systems . . ."

"I can't imagine getting you out of my system."

"I'm very keen to try," said Jessica with a laugh. "Because, frankly, I've been going crazy lusting after you."

Nathan gave a little laugh. He played for time by refocusing on his ice cream. Jessica could tell he was deliberating. He was such a good guy.

"I think you should stay over at my house tonight," he said, finally.

"I think so too," Jessica said, a huge grin breaking out across her face.

* * *

152

Jessica woke up the next morning with Nathan's arms wrapped around her.

"I should have known you'd be a cuddly sleeper," she muttered.

"Are you complaining?" Nathan said sleepily, pulling her in closer.

"No." Jessica took his hand in hers and idly stroked it. "Do you know what the time is?"

"Nope," said Nathan. "Go back to sleep."

"I have to go to the dance studio," Jessica explained.

"No, you don't, you're sick," insisted Nathan.

"I'm not sick!" Jessica laughed.

"You seem hot to me," said Nathan. She could sense him smiling.

Jessica reached out to the clock on the bedside table and turned it towards her. "I really have to go," she said. "I need to go to Mum and Dad's to get changed before the class."

"No," said Nathan, kissing her shoulders.

"I can come back later," Jessica said.

"I'm coming for dinner at your mum and dad's house, remember?"

"Oh yeah. Are you sure you're not sick and needing to stay home?"

"Are you offering to come and nurse me?"

"On second thoughts, I'll see you there," said Jessica. "You experiencing my dreadful nursing skills would put you off me for life."

She got out of bed and began searching for her discarded clothes.

"So, this is what your room is like . . ." Jessica observed. It was exactly as she'd imagined it: very neat and orderly, with minimal stuff.

"You saw it last night," pointed out Nathan.

"I was a little bit preoccupied last night . . . Can I just say, you were very inventive. My foot didn't hold you back at all."

"Right back at you. I think your dress is somewhere over by the wardrobe."

"Thanks."

Jessica located her clothes and pulled them on.

She went back over to the bed. "I'll see you later," she said, kissing him before hurrying out.

* * *

Jessica walked as fast as she could back to her parents' house, wondering if she'd be able to avoid bumping into her mum and dad as she slipped in. She was successful; it was a gorgeous morning, and she imagined they'd be enjoying breakfast in the garden. She crept along the hall and up the stairs and got changed into some shorts and a T-shirt ready to go to dance class. She couldn't wait until her cast was off and she was able to wear leggings again. She came down the stairs on her bottom rather than struggling with crutches and was grabbing her bag ready to go, when her mum called out, "There you are, Jessica!" from the kitchen.

Jessica turned. "Hi, Mum," she said. "I'm just on my way to the studio."

"We didn't hear you come home last night." Her mum had a twinkle in her eye.

"No, it was really late by the time we got back, so I stayed at Nathan's." Jessica could feel her cheeks turning crimson.

"That was very accommodating of him." Sarah was clearly trying not to laugh.

"Yes, anyway . . . I've got to go. I'll see you later."

"Will Nathan be joining us this evening?"

"Yes."

"Lovely, I must thank him for looking after you so well."

Jessica threw her mother a glare as she left.

* * *

"I went to Sadler's Wells last night," Jessica told Diana in a break between classes.

"How wonderful! What did you see?"

154

"The Bolshoi Ballet was performing their new *Swan Lake*. Their principal was excellent, though I think Petrov would have been a better choice to play Rothbart."

"You certainly know your ballet," commented Diana.

"I try to keep up with what's going on."

"Have you ever considered writing about it? Articles or blogs about the ballet world for people in the industry, but also for fans?"

"I read a few blogs from ballet dancers I like . . . I did have my own years ago and I loved writing posts for it, but never seemed to have the time to maintain it and it sort of fell by the wayside."

"You've got time now and you could also share your own experiences as well. Especially chronicling your recovery from your injury — I'm sure there are plenty of dancers who'd be interested in following that."

"It does sound fun."

"You could also review productions. You might even end up with some free tickets."

"Kind of like a catch-all for the ballet world?"

"Yes, everything you're interested in as well as your life."

"Thanks, Diana. That could be a really good idea."

* * *

For probably the first time in her life, Jessica's mind wasn't completely on the ballet practice she was a part of for the rest of the day. Part of it was thinking about what a fantastic time she'd had the night before and how her relationship with Nathan had changed, and part was going over what she could write about and how she could present it. She'd want to include plenty of photographs too . . . There were so many topics she would love to write about.

She finished at three and checked her phone — she had a message from Nathan. *Hoping you're having a good day. Missing you. x* She smiled and replied, *Missing you too. Just finished. What are you up to?*

His reply came through before she'd even finished packing up her bag: *Waiting for you.*

With a huge smile on her face, Jessica headed straight to Nathan's house.

* * *

A grumbling Jessica let herself into her parents' house three hours later with Nathan and Dennis at her side. "I can't believe you'd rather come here than stay in bed with me," she muttered to Nathan.

"You know that's not the case. It was nice of your parents to invite me and it would be rude not to turn up, especially as you live here."

"Goody two shoes."

"Hiya," said Sarah when they walked into the kitchen. She looked from one to the other of them, clearly checking to see if she could sense a difference between how they were behaving toward one another.

"Hello, Sarah, thanks for inviting me," said Nathan.

"My pleasure," Jessica's mother said. "And this must be Dennis." She knelt down to stroke Dennis's head. Monty came running in from the garden and was thrilled to discover his friend had arrived. So thrilled, that he managed to knock the kitchen bin over. Dennis was let off his lead and they went careering into the garden.

"Is there anything I can do to help?" Jessica asked her mum.

"Could you lay the table? Your brother and Molly are coming so we'll need to eat on the patio."

"Sure."

"I'll give you a hand," said Nathan.

They took cutlery and napkins outside where they found Joe putting away the lawnmower while the dogs got in his way.

"I get in trouble with Peter when he comes round if the grass is too long, apparently it messes up his football," Joe

156

said good-naturedly. "Did you have a good day at the studio, Jessica?"

"Yes, thanks, Dad."

"I thought you finished at three today?" he teased.

"I did . . . I went round to Nathan's for a bit afterwards."

"Oh right," Joe said, chuckling to himself as he went inside.

"Oh my God," said Jessica to Nathan. "I'm so sorry. They're not exactly subtle, are they?"

"No," said Nathan, frowning slightly.

"I haven't said anything to them," Jessica said quickly. "And I wasn't planning to. What's going on between us is just between us."

"I just feel a bit awkward, like your parents will think I'm taking advantage of you," Nathan explained.

"I'm thoroughly enjoying being taken advantage of," whispered Jessica.

Nathan opened his mouth to reply, but was interrupted by two little voices calling, "Auntie Jessica, Auntie Jessica," as Emily and Sophie came running out into the garden and flung themselves on their aunt.

Nathan gently supported her so she didn't topple over.

"Careful there, girls," he said. "Don't forget your aunt's still a bit broken."

"Sorry!" the girls chorused.

"Ballet class was so fun!" said Emily.

"Yeah, I'm definitely coming next week," added Sophie.

"That's great!" said Jessica.

Peter came out behind his sisters, clutching his precious football as usual.

"Would you play football with me, please, Nathan?" he asked.

"Sure. Girls, do you want to join?"

Emily and Sophie nodded.

Jessica watched as Nathan played with her nieces and nephew, who were soon joined by Monty and Dennis. He was right, it was potentially awkward that her mum and dad suspected what was going on between the two of them. She knew that they would judge it if they knew that neither Jessica nor Nathan wanted anything long-term. Nathan had already experienced the destruction of one long-distance relationship, and neither of them could commit to travelling back and forth regularly enough. When she was back in New York she had to be absolutely focused on her recovery — she couldn't divide herself. It had to be her career or Nathan.

CHAPTER TWELVE

"Are you all right?" Nathan asked as Jessica walked him and Dennis to the door at the end of the evening. Andrew and his family had left hours ago, but Nathan had hung around chatting with Jessica and her parents.

"Yeah," she said. "Just feeling a bit weird about what you said about my family knowing about us. You're right, it is awkward. But I don't know what to do about it."

"I don't think there's a lot we *can* do, really."

"Would you like us to stop . . . you know . . ." asked Jessica, doing everything she could to sound relaxed despite her stomach sinking at what she was suggesting. "And go back to just being friends?"

"No," he said, immediately. "Which is probably really selfish of me."

"I want to be selfish too, if that helps."

"I don't want you to have to hide anything and lie to your family."

"Neither do I, but I also don't want to deal with all their questions. I'm only going to be here for a few weeks." Jessica noticed the cloud fall on Nathan's face. "Let's make the most of our time together, privately."

"OK." Nathan sighed. "I suppose that makes sense, but I don't like it."

"Me neither, but I like it better than not getting to be with you, or explaining to my parents that I'm having a fling."

"Oh, I'm a fling, am I?" Nathan checked no one was around before pulling her to him for a kiss.

"The hottest fling of my life," Jessica whispered, her legs turning to jelly.

"I'll accept that," Nathan said. "I wish you could come home with me now."

"I know, but that really would give the game away," Jessica said regretfully.

"Can I see you tomorrow?"

"I could come round after you finish work?"

"I can't wait." Nathan gave her a final kiss goodbye. "Come on, Dennis, let's get you home."

* * *

Jessica's first thoughts when she woke up the next morning were of Nathan. She smiled, knowing she'd be seeing him later. She could hardly wait, but it seemed so far away.

It was like she had a need to be with Nathan. A need she'd never felt before. The only thing she could compare it to, she realised, was her need to dance, but that thought terrified her because she knew all too well that she couldn't have Nathan and her dance career. But there was no point in focusing on that, it wouldn't change anything. She should enjoy the time they had together while it lasted.

Jessica showered and dressed before going downstairs to have her morning coffee and breakfast. She was getting quite good at planning and saving herself trips up and down the stairs. It really was a pain having the only bathroom upstairs.

At some point she'd need to return to getting up earlier, she knew, but at the moment she was enjoying not forcing herself out of bed at 5 a.m. The extra rest was probably doing her body good anyway and helping it heal.

Her mum and dad had already gone to work in the estate agent's for the day and had left her a note to say they'd taken Monty with them, which didn't seem like the best of ideas. She made her breakfast while she debated what to do until she went to Nathan's.

Her mum's laptop was on the kitchen table and realising she had some time to kill, Jessica decided to make proper use of it. She messaged her mum to ask if she could use her computer. Sarah replied straight away that she could and so Jessica settled down in front of it with her yoghurt and fruit and began work.

* * *

Jessica was so engrossed in what she was doing that she completely lost track of time, looking up in surprise when she heard a key in the front door. It was already ten past one.

"Hello, love," said Sarah, coming into the kitchen with Monty. "I've popped home to make some lunch for your dad and me and to drop this horror off. He chewed through one of the printer cables. Thankfully it was turned off. I told your dad it wasn't a good idea to bring him in but I think he loves the idea of a dog snoring quietly away in a basket in the corner of the office."

"Oh dear!"

"Yes. Anyway, I've ordered a replacement cable. Is it all right if I leave Monty with you? I've taken him for a walk."

"Of course," said Jessica. "I'll be going out just after five though."

"That's fine, just leave him in the garden. I'll be home not long after that. Where are you going?" Sarah asked.

"Just round to Nathan's. I'd take Monty with me, but I can't manage him with my crutches."

"Nathan's again, eh?" commented her mother.

"Yeah, there's a video game we're playing together." It was the truth.

"A video game?"

"I know, it wouldn't usually be my kind of thing, but it's actually kind of fun."

"Have a good time. What are you working on there? You're looking very industrious."

Jessica turned the laptop around to face her mother. "I've set up a blog and newsletter on Substack."

"Centre Stage . . ." Sarah read out.

"Diana gave me the idea," Jessica explained. "I've followed ballet blogs for years, and ran my own for a while, but I was just talking about my own career on it and I didn't keep it up. Diana suggested I write about my recovery and ballet news as well. I thought I'd also make some videos of basic techniques to post on there once my foot's healed."

"That's a brilliant idea — and I love the layout."

"Thanks, I'm hoping that if it takes off, I might be paid to write articles for other blogs or magazines, or get sponsored to review products maybe . . . It's something I can do while my foot heals, anyway."

Sarah gave her daughter a hug. "Well done, darling. Let me know if there's anything I can do to help."

"Actually . . ." Jessica said.

* * *

Sarah headed off back to the estate agent's an hour later armed with sandwiches for her husband and having completed an impromptu photo shoot for her daughter in the garden.

Jessica told Monty firmly to behave himself and got back on the laptop, uploading the pictures her mum had taken, and then went through her phone to find some more of her dancing.

The afternoon passed as quickly as the morning had, with Jessica only stopping to refill her coffee cup. Monty generally stayed by her feet, wandering into the garden for a sunbathe occasionally when he got bored.

Aware of how engrossed she was, she set an alarm on her phone for five. As much as she was enjoying working on her Substack blog, she was looking forward to seeing Nathan even more.

She brushed her hair and reapplied her make-up and then headed off to Nathan's house, taking a detour via the supermarket to pick up some snacks for them.

Nathan opened his door almost as soon as she'd knocked.

"How was work?" she asked when they finally pulled apart.

"A bizarre number of ingrowing toenails today," said Nathan, laughing. "What have you been up to?"

"I've been starting a Substack!" Jessica declared. "About ballet and being a ballerina, basically. Can I show it to you?"

"Absolutely." Nathan smiled broadly at her evident excitement. "Let me turn my laptop on."

He put his laptop on the kitchen table and logged in. "I'll grab us a couple of beers while you get it up."

Jessica pulled up what she'd done, and Nathan came up behind her, kissing her on her neck before focusing on the screen.

"That looks brilliant," he said as she showed him the fruits of her labour. "Really professional. I like the design you've used."

"Thank you," Jessica said. "I'm hoping to make it appeal to ballet lovers as well as people who dance."

"That's a gorgeous photo," Nathan commented, hovering the mouse over a professional photograph of Jessica taken during a performance of *Giselle*. "It doesn't look like you, though."

"I've got a lot of stage make-up on in that, and my hair's got so much product in it wouldn't move if I was in a hurricane!"

"I like you best with your hair down like you had it on Saturday night," said Nathan, kissing her neck.

"Noted," replied Jessica, pulling her hair out of the ponytail it was up in.

Nathan smiled. "Do you want to go out to eat?" he asked.

"Nah." Jessica shook her head. "I just want to hang out with you here. I can't do so many of the things I want to do to you if we're in public."

"That sounds very good to me," said Nathan.

* * *

As much as Jessica would have liked to stay the night with Nathan, her parents' suspicions about the two of them would go into overdrive if she did, so they reluctantly said goodbye to each other at ten. Nathan and Dennis insisted upon walking her home, which was lovely but meant they couldn't say the goodbye they wanted to in case someone was watching.

Sarah and Joe were still up watching television in the sitting room.

"Hi, love," Sarah called. "Come in here, we've got something to tell you."

Jessica came into the sitting room and smiled at the sight of her mum and dad holding hands on the sofa.

"What is it?" Jessica said. "You two look like naughty school kids."

"Your dad's taking me away for the bank holiday next weekend!" said Sarah. "We're leaving as soon as your dad finishes work on Friday and we're going to a country hotel near Oxford for three nights!"

"How lovely!" said Jessica. She couldn't remember her parents ever going away for a weekend together when she was growing up. Probably because of all her dance commitments and them needing to drive her around all the time.

"It's going to be so fancy!" Sarah said.

"You deserve a treat," said Joe, clearly thrilled with how well his surprise had gone down.

"So, you'll be coming back on Monday?"

"Yes, Monday evening. We've got a National Trust property to visit on the way home," Sarah said.

Three whole nights and days with Nathan, Jessica thought to herself gleefully.

Sarah's face fell. "Oh no! I've just thought of something," she said. She hurried out of the room and returned with her pocket diary. "I promised I'd babysit the children on Monday! Andrew and Molly are going walking and for lunch with some friends — they asked me ages ago. I can't let them down."

"I can do it," Jessica found herself saying.

"Are you sure?" asked Molly, managing to sound both hopeful and doubtful. "It's the whole day."

"Of course," Jessica replied. "It's the bank holiday so there aren't any dance classes, and I've promised to take the kids to the cinema sometime anyway. We'll have a great time."

She tried not to be put out by the look she caught between her mum and dad. She'd never looked after her nieces and nephew before, she got that, and her having them for a whole day wasn't an ideal introduction.

"I'll be fine," she said, firmly.

"All right, then," said Sarah. "Thank you."

Jessica went into the kitchen to make a coffee, proud of herself for stepping up to help her family, even if she wasn't quite sure what she was going to do for the entirety of a day with three children.

More importantly, though: three whole days and nights with Nathan! Well, three nights and two days, technically, now that she was spending Monday babysitting. She messaged him while the kettle boiled: *My parents are going away for the bank holiday weekend. Can Monty and I come and stay?*

He replied immediately. *Of course! That is the best news I have ever heard.*

Inspiration hit Jessica: *There's only one condition.*

Anything, Nathan replied.

You need to help me look after Peter, Emily and Sophie all day on Monday.

Challenge accepted.

* * *

Jessica and Monty were waiting with their bags on Nathan's doorstep when he got home from work on Friday. He greeted Jessica with a kiss and Monty with a pat on the head.

They retrieved Dennis from inside the house and Nathan drove them to the canal so the dogs could have a run where it was flat for Jessica on her crutches. Jessica grinned, recalling the day they'd spent canoeing there, back before they'd admitted how much they liked each other.

"You're remembering me falling into the canal, aren't you?" Nathan accused her, noticing the delight on her face.

"Not exactly . . . More you driving home topless *after* you'd fallen in the canal."

"It's no wonder you couldn't resist me." Nathan stopped her and gently tilted her chin up. "You are wonderful, Jessica Stone." And he kissed her.

***

Saturday and Sunday flew by. Jessica's face ached from smiling and laughing so much. But there was part of her that knew she needed to be careful. This fling was not getting flung and the more time she spent with Nathan, the more she liked him and the harder it was going to be when she had to leave him.

They were so different in so many ways, but they seemed to fit together. She loved spending time with him and the more she got to know him, the more she realised what a great guy he was.

Jessica had been having so much fun she barely had time to worry about babysitting her nieces and nephew, but she woke up in full panic mode on Monday morning.

"How on earth am I going to entertain three children for the whole day?" she moaned, hiding under the duvet. "What do they even like to do? We're picking them up at ten and Andrew and Molly won't be back until seven — that's nine whole hours to fill up! The cinema's only going to be like two hours! We've got seven hours to fill with fun stuff! It can't be done!"

Nathan laughed, and joined her under the duvet, spooning around her. "Don't worry. It'll be fine," he said. "We'll pick them up and go to the park with the dogs. Then we'll drop the dogs off and take them to McDonald's for lunch and to the supermarket to choose some sweets before going to the cinema. I've booked tickets for the two o'clock showing."

"You looked up the showings for me!"

"Yeah. I figured you'd be freaking out so thought that was one thing I could organise."

"Thank you."

"So that'll take us up to about four o'clock. We'll come back here to get the dogs, and Molly said they all really like crafts so we can do some of that."

"We can't just 'do crafts'," pointed out Jessica. "We need craft materials."

"I have two nieces, remember?" said Nathan. "And they come to stay occasionally. I have a full craft cupboard in the spare bedroom upstairs. I added mug painting kits for us all."

"Oh my goodness, you are amazing!" cried Jessica.

"Yes, I am. And then they can play *LEGO Star Wars* on the Xbox while we make them some pizza for tea. See? Nine hours filled up no problem. Now, I've got a little something I want to do to you before the madness begins," he said.

* * *

Jessica was exhausted and her foot ached, but she had to admit Nathan had been right: the day had gone by really quickly, and everyone had had a good time. Peter, Emily and Sophie were playing video games with Nathan while the pizzas cooked and Jessica made a salad which the children would no doubt ignore, but she would enjoy.

Nathan appeared in the doorway. "They seem happy in there so I thought I'd come to check on you. Do you need any painkillers?"

"I've already taken some, thanks," said Jessica. "It's not too bad and it's been a brilliant day."

"Good. They're great kids."

"You're fantastic with them."

Nathan shrugged. "I've spent a lot of time with my own nieces."

"How old are they?"

"Four and six, like Emily and Sophie."

"What are they like?"

"Mia, she's six, is just like my sister. She can talk anyone into anything. Her little sister, Rosie, follows her around everywhere."

"Do you want children?" Jessica found herself asking. She wasn't sure why she did or if she even wanted to know the answer. It was no business of hers anyway. She was leaving soon. It's not like she was ever going to have his babies.

"Yes," said Nathan.

"That's very definite," said Jessica.

"I want a family. For me, that's important. Do you?"

"Honestly, I don't know," Jessica admitted. "I guess I've never really thought about it properly. It was always something I might do at some point."

"It's a pretty big 'something'," commented Nathan.

"Yep. The thing is, I'm not even sure I'd be a very good mother," Jessica shared. "I'm a pretty useless aunt."

"The kids seem to like you."

"Yeah, because I took them to McDonald's and the cinema!"

"I saw Sophie climb up onto your lap during the movie."

"That was cute."

"She wouldn't have done that if she didn't like and trust you."

"I guess not," she said. "I'm enjoying spending more time with them. I know I was nervous about today, but it's been really fun. Thank you for organising so much of it and driving us around."

"Not a problem, though they've completely worn me out! I don't know how your brother and Molly do it."

"Me too! I'm going to fall into bed tonight."

"I'll miss you in my bed," said Nathan, bending down and kissing her lips.

"I'll miss you too," said Jessica smiling.

Nathan checked the pizzas. "I think these are done. I'll tell the horde."

Jessica's phone rang in her pocket. Distracted, and thinking it was probably Molly wondering how everything was, she answered it quickly, not checking who was calling.

"Hi, Jessica!" said the familiar voice of her friend Bethany. "I haven't heard from you for ages and I had like literally five minutes between rehearsals so thought I'd call and have a quick catch-up. I've missed you! How's that poor foot?"

"Hi, Bethany, it's good to hear from you. Give me just a second." Jessica's gut wrenched at the reminder of what she was missing out on in New York. The children came into the kitchen with Nathan. Jessica gestured to her phone and hobbled out on one crutch into the sitting room for some quiet.

"Sorry about that," Jessica said, resuming the phone conversation. "I'm looking after my nephew and nieces today. My foot's still sore, still in plaster."

"What a pain for you. Still, at least you get a rest," said Bethany. "We're all so exhausted. Jean-Paul is pushing us so hard with the choreography. Gabriel has been in an absolute grump for the last week."

Jessica knew her friend wasn't being intentionally hurtful, but it was really hard to hear what she was missing out on. It should be her dealing with Gabriel's strops and complaining about Jean-Paul. "Any idea when you'll be back?" Bethany continued. "It feels like you've been gone for ever and I could really do with your help with the Rose Adage — it's a bit of a mess at the moment."

"Sorry, I'm not sure. I haven't rebooked my flight yet. But I'll let you know when I do. I'd better go. I think one of my nieces needs me," she lied.

Jessica felt guilty. It was such an exciting opportunity for her friend and she wanted to support her, but she didn't think she could keep up her cheerful tone any longer.

"OK! I'll message you some footage and maybe you could send me some feedback," said Bethany. "Bye!"

Jessica turned her phone off and went back into the kitchen, attempting to plaster a smile on her face.

"What's the matter?" asked Nathan as soon as she stepped into the room.

"Nothing," Jessica said. "I'm fine. It was my friend calling from New York." She sat down at the table and began serving herself with food.

Nathan was distracted by Sophie calling out, "Look, Nathan! I can fit a whole slice of pizza in my mouth in one go!"

But Jessica noticed Nathan kept a careful eye on her for the rest of the meal.

* * *

The phone call from Bethany had reignited Jessica's determination that she would dance professionally again, as soon as possible.

Bethany messaged the videos as promised. Her friend had been right that she needed help with the Rose Adage — she was struggling with the extended balances en pointe, and while the rest of her technique was good, her performance lacked emotion and the spark that would hook the audience. This was something Jessica knew she could help with, even if it would be far easier to do so in person. She took meticulous notes and messaged her friend back, offering a video call in the dance studio so she could give her some direct feedback.

Jessica knew that she had to be very careful with her foot, but she upped the exercise she was doing with the other parts of her body, breaking up her exercise routines with working on her blog.

She wrote a blog post about her injury, not about how she was staying in shape or her rehab, she'd write that later, but about the mental impact an injury could have on a dancer. How emotional it felt not to be able to do the things you loved most in the world, and not to know whether you'd ever be able to dance at the same level again. She was close to tears as she hit publish, but she was really pleased she'd done it; it felt cathartic to get her feelings out there and she hoped that maybe her post might help someone else who was struggling to understand that they weren't alone.

* * *

Jessica was finishing off a kettlebell workout in her mum and dad's sitting room a couple of days later when her phone started ringing. She glanced down at it and saw Bethany's name flashing on the screen. She ignored it. She felt bad. She wanted to support her friend, but it was still hard not to feel jealous and resentful sometimes, especially when she was exercising as best as she could with her injury. She'd call her back later. She really wasn't in the mood to talk now. A moment later a notification showed up that she had a voice-mail message. She completed her workout and then listened to it:

"Hi, babe, it's Bethany. Why didn't you tell me you have a Substack? Your post about dance injuries is being shared all over Instagram! We all love it!"

Jessica had set up an Instagram account when she'd first started her Substack. She'd shared some dancing photos on there, but hadn't really done anything else with it other than posting links in a story to each Substack post when they went live. She opened the Instagram app on her phone, her heart in her mouth.

Her followers had gone up from twenty-six to over a thousand, and when she clicked on her notifications, she saw her latest post had been shared more than five thousand times, including by the Miami City Ballet! She quickly logged on to her blog and found hundreds of comments waiting for her.

There were some from ballet dancers she didn't know, some from ballet lovers, many of whom had seen her perform over the years, and even a few from members of her own company, wishing her a speedy recovery and telling her how much she was missed. She felt her eyes well up. She doubted she'd cried as much in the whole of her life previously as she had in the past few weeks.

She texted Nathan immediately. He was at work so she knew he couldn't see it straight away but he was the person she most wanted to share her good news with.

Then she gave herself a stern talking-to about how she was treating Bethany, who'd always been supportive of her. The role of Aurora was gone for Jessica and there was nothing she could do about that, but she could help her friend more than she had been. And who knows, working with Bethany on her technique might help Jessica with her own dancing in the future.

She messaged her friend to arrange a time for the video call she'd promised and suggested they do something like that regularly until Jessica was back in New York.

* * *

Time flew by in a way that Jessica would never have imagined it could when she'd first hurt her foot. With working at the dance studio, writing her increasingly popular Substack posts, exercising, spending time with her family, and seeing as much of Nathan as she could, her days felt full and busy in a way that seemed to fulfil rather than drain her.

Although she still hadn't said anything directly to her parents about her relationship with Nathan, she knew they approved of him and they encouraged her to spend the night at his house claiming they didn't like the idea of her walking home by herself late at night. Jessica was more than willing to go along with this. She couldn't deny that her feelings for Nathan were getting stronger — she loved being with him. Thinking about how soon she'd be returning to New York was something she tried very hard not to do.

Things between Jessica and her parents were also probably the best they'd ever been. Not that they'd ever had a terrible relationship, but being so focused on her goals meant Jessica hadn't spent much time just being with them, especially since leaving home. It was nice to get to know them more. She was getting along really well with both of them, but especially her mum. Sarah was so supportive of her blog, even proofreading Jessica's posts for her and forwarding the links once they were live to everyone she knew.

Jessica had a surprise when she needed some old photos for her Substack and her mum disappeared for a while, returning with two boxes full of anything and everything to do with Jessica's dancing. They contained newspaper clippings, photos, ticket stubs, and programmes, dating back to her first performance well over twenty years ago.

"I had no idea you'd kept all this," exclaimed Jessica, looking through the top layers of one of the boxes.

"Of course," Sarah said with a shrug.

"How did you even get hold of some of these programmes? This one's from Berlin — you didn't come to any of those performances."

"I tracked any down online that I couldn't get in person."

"Wow. Thank you, this is great. A lot of this will be really useful."

"Just be careful with them! Make sure your hands are clean."

"They are, Mum," Jessica reassured. "I'm really touched that you've got all this. There's stuff here I'm sure I've never seen."

"My daughter is brilliant," said Sarah, getting up and giving Jessica a kiss on the forehead. "It's only natural I'd want to collect evidence of this."

* * *

Jessica was walking back home with her mum one Saturday after they'd been shopping together when she saw the all too familiar figure of Mrs Edith White bustling towards them. Her heart sank.

"Ah, Jessica," Mrs White said once she was closer, "I see you've been forced to hang around here for longer than you'd planned."

"Yes, it would seem so," bristled Jessica, her good mood rapidly evaporating. She felt her forehead furrow.

"I imagine you're appreciating your family now you need them to look after you."

Before Jessica could manage to formulate a response, she heard her mother say, "Jessica has always appreciated us!" It was in the voice she usually reserved for particularly difficult Year 6s.

Clearly ruffled, Mrs White said, "Well, I only meant that maybe she'll visit more . . ."

"Jessica has just been promoted to principal ballerina in one of the top ballet companies in the world. She's based in New York which doesn't make it very easy for her to pop in for a cuppa. She comes home when she can and we're very proud of her."

"I'm sure you are," muttered Mrs White, continuing on her way rather more quickly than usual.

Jessica and Sarah watched her go.

"I can't believe you said that, Mum!" Jessica was in awe.

"Neither can I," admitted Sarah. "I expect I'll pay for it at the next WI meeting."

"Thank you," Jessica said, as her mum opened the front door to her parents' home and they went inside. "For standing up for me, I mean."

Sarah shrugged. "I know you don't really need anyone to stand up for you, but I couldn't help it."

"Are you really proud of me?" Jessica asked quietly.

Sarah put down the shopping and turned to face her daughter. "Of course we're proud of you. How can you doubt that?"

"I know you've got all those programmes and photos from my performances, but you never seem very . . . excited when I try to tell you about my work. It sort of feels like you think it's a waste of time."

"Oh my goodness, no! But I guess it's hard for me to understand how you feel about dancing. It's so . . . all-consuming for you."

Jessica nodded. "It is."

"When you were six, your dad was worried you'd wear yourself out with all the dancing you were doing. I told him you'd be bored with it soon, that it was just a phase. I guess I was wrong."

"I love ballet, Mum, and I'm not ready to give it up yet. But I also love you guys so much. And I have missed you all. I didn't realise how much I missed you until I stopped dancing for long enough to take a proper look at my life. It's been brilliant spending time with you, just little things like going for a coffee together, or popping in to see Dad at work."

"I've really enjoyed it too," said Sarah, giving her daughter a hug.

"I promise I'll be back to visit again more often than I have been. I was thinking that maybe I could sublet my apartment during the off-season and stay with you. Perhaps I could work for Diana. I'd be able to help Andrew and Molly with the kids."

"That would be wonderful," Sarah said looking delighted. "Let's not talk about you going just yet, though — we've still got you for a little while longer. Your dad and I think what you do is amazing, but we do miss our daughter a lot and it's been so lovely having you here. And I know we're not the only people who think so . . . "

* * *

The day when Jessica's cast could officially come off, 15 September, finally arrived. She'd called the hospital a month ago to arrange it, and had managed to make an appointment for that morning; she didn't want to spend a moment more with her foot in plaster than she needed to. She had been warned, though, that if the X-ray showed the bone wasn't healed, she'd need to keep the cast on for longer.

Her mum and dad were both at work. Her dad had offered to take the morning off to come with her, but Jessica had said she'd be fine taking the bus and had promised she'd get a taxi home if her foot was sore. The person she really wanted with her was Nathan, but he would also be at work for the day, though he was coming round to her parents' house for what would hopefully be a celebratory supper that evening.

Jessica was getting ready to go. She was so nervous about how her foot would be that her hands shook as she put her earrings in. The doorbell went.

Monty jumped up and began barking, running to the front door, and she followed him, holding onto his collar as she opened the door and found Nathan on the step.

"What are you doing here?" she asked. "Why aren't you at work?"

"I took the day off," he said simply. "I wanted to come with you to the hospital. Another one of the doctors is covering my appointments."

"Can you do that?"

"Even doctors get days off," said Nathan. "I booked it as holiday when you first made the appointment. I didn't tell you before because I knew you'd insist you'd be fine by yourself."

"I probably would have," Jessica confessed. "But I'm really glad you're coming."

"I hoped you would be," said Nathan, kissing her. "Are you almost ready to go?"

"Yep."

"Nervous?"

"Definitely," said Jessica with a little smile.

* * *

Jessica was sent to have her foot X-rayed once they'd arrived at the hospital. Everything seemed to take for ever and she struggled not to show her frustration. She was grateful to Nathan for his calming presence as he chatted to her, got her a coffee, and rested his hand on her knee when her leg bounced up and down as her nerves got the better of her. She waited anxiously for the doctor to check the X-ray and give her the verdict.

Finally, her name was called.

"Would you like me to come in with you?" Nathan asked quietly.

"Yes, please," Jessica whispered back as she stood up to go into the examination room.

"Hello, Jessica," said a tall, middle-aged man, closing the door behind them. "I'm Dr Chung. I've had a look at your X-ray, and I'm happy to take the cast off today."

Jessica let out a sigh of relief.

"I take it you haven't enjoyed having your foot in plaster?" joked Dr Chung.

"Not really," said Jessica.

"I've got some sheets here with some exercises you should do to strengthen the foot. It will still be a bit sore, and I'll prescribe you some painkillers for that. You'll need to be careful not to overdo it for a while."

"How soon before I can start exercising on it properly?" Jessica asked. "I'm a dancer, and I'd like to be able to get back to work as soon as possible."

"You'll need to build up slowly," said Dr Chung. "Would you like a referral to a physiotherapist? It could take a little while."

"No, thank you," said Jessica. "I live in New York and my company will sort me out with one of their sports physiotherapists when I go back."

"OK, great. Let's get this cast off then," Dr Chung said.

He called a nurse in and Jessica climbed up onto the examination table. Nathan stayed by her and held her hand. A wave of nausea came over her as the nurse started up the saw, and she flinched when he cut through the plaster. She couldn't tear her eyes away from her foot as the saw worked its way along the cast.

The nurse stopped the saw and gently removed the cast. Jessica saw her foot for the first time in six weeks.

Her foot looked tiny and skeletal. It was pale and covered in flakes of skin. It looked weak. She burst into tears.

"It's OK," said Nathan, holding her. "It's OK."

"It's not OK," said Jessica, pushing him away. She knew she was being unfair, but she didn't want to hear someone telling her things were fine. Things were not fine. The doctor had been positive, and she'd been very aware that she'd need to rebuild the muscles in her foot, but, right now, she couldn't imagine ever being able to go en pointe again. She needed someone to understand how terrifying that thought was for her, not to tell her that everything was fine.

"Are you all done?" Jessica asked the nurse as she furiously wiped at her eyes.

"Yes," said the nurse, kindly. "Would you like a wheelchair to help you out?"

"No, thank you," said Jessica. There was no way she was going to get back in a wheelchair again. She put on the spare sock she'd packed in her bag, but didn't feel confident enough to try a shoe. She climbed off the table, ignoring Nathan's offer of help, and picked up her crutches.

"Let's go," she said, before adding, "Thank you," to the nurse.

* * *

"Are you all right?" asked Nathan, hurrying to keep up with her as Jessica raced down the hospital corridors on her crutches.

Jessica stopped. "Of course I'm not all right," she snapped. "How could I possibly be all right?"

"I've seen feet in a lot worse condition when a cast has just been taken off," soothed Nathan. "It'll look a lot better after a good soak in a bath and some moisturiser."

Jessica took a deep breath. She didn't want to argue with Nathan, and she appreciated that he was only trying to be nice. It wasn't his fault that he didn't understand.

"You're right," she said. "Thanks."

Nathan drove Jessica back to his place. They spent the journey in silence, plans for her rehabilitation going round and round Jessica's head.

Nathan parked in his driveway and came around to help Jessica out.

"What do you want to do for the rest of the day?" Nathan asked, handing her her crutches.

"Actually," Jessica said, "would you mind if I headed off? That bath sounds like a really good idea and I sort of want to be by myself for a while."

Jessica felt really bad to be blowing Nathan off, especially as he'd booked the day off — but she needed to be alone right now. She needed to have a wallow and then work out how she was going to get herself literally back on her feet.

"Shall I drive you around?"

"No, thanks. I'll walk. With the crutches," she quickly added, seeing the concern on Nathan's face.

"OK," said Nathan. "I'll see you for dinner tonight."

"Of course," said Jessica, forcing a smile. There was no way out of it, but the last thing she felt like doing was attending a celebratory supper for herself.

She reached up and kissed him. She hated leaving him when things still weren't right between them, but he just didn't understand what she was going through.

Jessica began walking but stopped when she got to the turning to the dance school and found herself heading towards it.

The door was locked, and she let herself in with the key Diana had given her and turned on the lights. She walked to the barre and laid down her crutches. Slowly, and very cautiously, she put her feet into first and began working her way up the positions.

Her foot seemed to handle that, so she moved on to some simple exercises, too nervous to really enjoy herself, but grateful she was able to at least do some dancing.

She was so absorbed in her movements that she didn't hear Diana come in until her old teacher began clapping.

Jessica turned and gave her a shy smile.

"Your cast is off!" said Diana. "How wonderful!"

"It is," said Jessica, slowly. "And I know I should be really happy, but all I can think about is how much work there is ahead of me and what I'll do if my foot isn't as strong as it was before."

"Has any doctor given you any impression that your foot won't heal fully?" asked Diana kindly.

"No," admitted Jessica.

"And you haven't seen a physiotherapist yet, have you?"

"No," said Jessica, a smile returning to her face.

"Then I would save your worrying until after you see a physio at least."

"My company will arrange for me to see their dance physios, but that means I have to be back in New York," Jessica explained.

"And you don't want to go back?" guessed Diana.

"I'm completely torn," said Jessica. "I can't wait to get back to work, but I've also really enjoyed spending more time with my family, and getting to know Nathan." She felt herself blushing.

"You can't be in two places at the same time, so it seems to me like you've got a decision to make."

* * *

Monty was pleased to see Jessica when she let herself into her parents' house. She made herself some lunch, very gingerly standing on her foot. It was sore, but nothing like it had been. She could hardly wait to begin training carefully on it, but she'd need to have it checked over by a dance physio first. That would mean going back to New York. She couldn't afford a private consultation if she stayed in the UK and she didn't want to waste more time waiting for a referral to come through for a physiotherapist who was unlikely to be a dance expert.

As for her family, she'd miss them all terribly. She wouldn't be performing over Christmas, though, thanks to her foot, so she'd be able to come back for at least a couple of weeks then while everyone else was dancing *The Nutcracker*. She couldn't remember the last time she'd taken a break at Christmas.

But what about Nathan? They'd been together for such a short amount of time, and they'd both agreed that this was just a fling. She understood that Nathan wasn't ready for anything serious after his divorce, and they lived on different continents. But even if they did live closer together, Nathan didn't understand what ballet meant to her. She couldn't be with someone like that. She had to give even more of herself to her career now so that she could get her fitness back to what it had been. She didn't have time for a relationship. Not unless she was going to give up on her dreams.

And the longer she stayed here, the more she could feel herself falling in love with Nathan, no matter how many times she told herself that he wasn't right for her. The more it was dragged out, the worse it would be when she left.

She'd made her decision. She logged into her iPad and rebooked her flight for the next day.

* * *

Jessica debated whether to leave telling Nathan until after dinner or even the next morning. But he'd be at work tomorrow, and she felt she'd be being dishonest if she went through the evening without saying anything.

Are you home? she messaged, and when he replied that he was, she headed back over to his house, leaving a very sad Monty behind.

* * *

"Hey, it's good to see you again," said Nathan, opening the door and kissing her. "Come in. How's your foot feeling?"

"Pretty good," said Jessica. "I thought I should use the crutches to come over here, but I managed a few ballet exercises on it earlier. Very gentle ones," she added when she saw him start to frown.

Reassured, Nathan grinned. "I bet it felt amazing to dance again."

"It did, but it also made me even more aware of how much strengthening it needs."

"Sure," Nathan said. "You're doing all the right stuff, though."

"I hope so." Jessica forced a little smile.

"What do you feel like doing?" Nathan asked, running his hand down her arm.

Jessica took a deep breath. "I need to talk to you," she said.

"This sounds ominous. Let's go through to the kitchen," he replied.

Jessica followed him, her stomach in knots.

"Coffee?" he asked.

"No, thanks." She wanted to get this over and done with and not drag it out by making hot drinks.

Nathan sat down opposite her, seeming to know it wasn't the time to sit beside her, legs touching, like they usually did.

"So, what did you want to talk about?"

"I'm flying back to America tomorrow," Jessica said.

"Oh."

"I wanted to tell you before tonight because, well, I'm so grateful for everything you've done for me. The time we've spent together has meant such a lot to me."

"It can't have meant that much to you if you're disappearing as soon as you've got the cast off your foot," said Nathan, quietly.

"I need to get back to work," she explained.

"You can't exercise here?" he asked, not meeting her eye.

"I could, but my company has better facilities than Diana has. They have a fully equipped gym and specialist dance physiotherapists. It's the best place for me to be to get back into shape."

Nathan was silent. "Hey," Jessica said, reaching out to hold his hand. "We both knew this was just a short-term thing. It's what we both agreed to."

"What if it turned into a long-term thing?" Nathan muttered.

"Nathan, we'll have an ocean between us, and I'm going to be working flat out to prove to my company that I can be as good as I was."

182

"You don't have time to have a relationship with me?"

"I wouldn't put it like that. You have a full-time job too," reasoned Jessica. She hated seeing the hurt on Nathan's face and not being able to do anything to stop it. But there was no point in her agreeing to continue anything. It simply wouldn't be logistically possible.

"I'm capable of stepping away from my job," said Nathan.

"My job isn't one that I can step away from," Jessica responded hotly. "Not yet, anyway."

"I've made room in my life for you."

"I know you did," said Jessica. Realisation hit her. "I'm not Claire," she said. "This isn't just about the fact that I'm work obsessed."

"I know you're not Claire," said Nathan. "But you're another woman choosing her job over me."

Jessica got up and walked over to him. She put her arms around him and put her head on his shoulder. "You said you weren't ready for a relationship, remember?"

"I did say something stupid like that."

"You're only just divorced."

"I know, and that was how I felt when I first helped you up from the ground after you fell . . . but now . . ."

Jessica looked at him for a moment, seeing the hurt in his eyes. "It's just not the right time for us," she said sadly.

CHAPTER THIRTEEN

Jessica had been back in New York for two months, and it didn't feel any more like home than it had when she'd arrived exhausted after her flight and struggled up the three flights of stairs to her apartment, dragging her suitcase behind her. It was definitely colder in her little attic rooms now, and it kind of made her miss the ridiculous heat of the summer.

She pulled herself out of bed when her alarm went off at 6 a.m., which she'd decided was quite early enough for her to start each day, and headed straight for the shower before pulling on her leotard, yoga pants, a T-shirt and a hoodie.

She ate a bowl of porridge with berries and protein powder mixed in and finished packing her bag with snacks and water.

It was Friday, and she was looking forward to the weekend. She was going to do some actual sightseeing. It was criminal that there were so many places in this amazing city that she'd never seen because she hadn't had the time. She was making some time now but she couldn't help wishing that Nathan was here to share it with her. He would be a fun sightseeing companion.

She thought back to when she'd last seen him, sat at his kitchen table, his head in his hands as she left. He'd made his excuses and hadn't come to supper that night. Jessica understood, but she hated that that image was the last she had of him. She wondered every day how he was doing. She'd wanted to message or call him a thousand times, but it wouldn't be fair on either of them. A clean break was easier, or at least that's what she'd told herself in the beginning. It didn't seem to have proven itself true yet.

Shaking her head to clear the image of Nathan from her mind, Jessica made sure the alarm was set in her phone to call her dad later; it was his birthday, and she had a surprise for him that she couldn't wait to reveal. Then she headed out of her apartment, treading lightly on the stairs.

She was still cautious of her foot, but her company's physiotherapist, combined with a very careful and intensive exercise routine, had worked wonders. Jessica had insisted that she couldn't return to full training until the New Year, despite the pressure put on her by some of the instructors. She wouldn't rush her healing. It was good to be taking part in company classes again, though, and she'd made an effort to attempt to make some new friends. There was no denying that she was part of a very competitive industry, but helping Bethany had shown her that she didn't need to always see other dancers as the enemy. She'd spent her whole career being guarded and wary when in reality they could help and support each other. On *The Sleeping Beauty*'s opening night, Jessica had sent a huge bouquet of flowers to be delivered to her friend's dressing room and she'd been in the front row, cheering Bethany on.

Jessica walked to the dance studio, dodging puddles from the heavy overnight showers. She checked the noticeboard in the hallway out of habit and found herself an empty studio. She put on her music and then began making her way through her exercises. She'd recently begun pointe work again and was pleased with her progress.

Feeling confident she could push herself more, she moved into the middle of the room and began Aurora's Act 1 variation. Her body was overtaken by Tchaikovsky's score as it stretched and spun. She could feel her movements were almost back to pre-injury, her muscles relaxed and supple. She ended and heard applause.

She looked up and saw Nathan. Her heart leapt, but she somehow forced herself not to run into his arms. As thrilled as she was to see him, she had to protect herself, and she couldn't hurt him any more than she had already.

She didn't know what to say so was grateful when Nathan spoke. "That was beautiful," he said, quietly. He had a suitcase by his feet.

"Thank you," Jessica replied. "How . . . how did you get in?"

"I fed the doorman a sob story about a guy travelling across the world to speak to one of their ballerinas."

Jessica's heart gave a little jolt. "What are you doing here?"

"I missed you," he said simply.

"I missed you too. You've travelled a long way to tell me that."

"I've got some other stuff to say as well."

"OK," said Jessica.

"Can you take a break and come for a coffee with me?"

"Sure," she replied, trying to act as unfazed by this turn of events as possible, even though her stomach was flipping like crazy at just the sight of him. This had definitely not been part of her plans.

Jessica pulled her hoodie and tracksuit bottoms back on and they walked in silence out of the building. Jessica noticed Nathan getting a few appreciative glances from the other dancers arriving and automatically moved closer to him.

"It's so good to see you walking without crutches," Nathan commented as Jessica directed him towards her favourite coffee shop.

"It feels good," she said.

"Grab a table. Your usual?" he said when they entered the blissfully warm haven, filled with the smell of pastries and coffee beans.

186

Jessica nodded and sat down at her favourite table for two by the window, and Nathan soon returned with two black Americanos.

"So," Jessica said, "what have you come all the way here to tell me?"

"That I love you," said Nathan, calmly taking a sip of his drink like they were just passing the time of day. "But I need to build up to that bit." His eyes were seemingly determined to avoid hers.

Jessica stared at him open-mouthed while he continued, trying to quickly process what was happening rationally and not fling herself at him. They'd both been hurt, and she didn't want that to happen again. She wasn't sure her heart could handle it.

"I've been watching videos of you performing," Nathan admitted. "I needed to understand why ballet meant so much to you, why you've devoted so much of your life to it. And I think I do now, at least a little. When you dance, you're . . . mesmerising," he said. "I couldn't leave things as they were between us, and the more I thought about it, the more I realised how much I wanted to be with you. I can handle playing second fiddle to your dancing."

"You would never be in second place," Jessica said, meeting Nathan's eyes. "I promise you that. But I'm not ready to give up dancing yet."

"I understand that, and I don't want you to," he said. "Ballet is a huge part of you, and it has to be completely your decision when you decide to retire. I can move here. I've been looking into it . . ."

"I don't think that would be a very good idea," she said gently, trying to control her emotions as her heart beat wildly in her chest.

Nathan's face fell and he broke eye contact. "I promise you, I'm completely over Claire. I realise now that if we'd been right for each other, we would have made our marriage work, no matter where she needed to travel for her work."

"I think that's very true, and no, it's not because of Claire. I believe you if you say you're over her," Jessica said.

"Then if it's too much too soon . . ." he began, his gaze returning to hers.

"No, it's not that," Jessica said, trying to hide the smile from her face. "It wouldn't be a good idea because I'm moving back to the UK."

"What?"

"I've been miserable here without you and my family, mainly you, if I'm being completely honest." Jessica felt the relief of finally being able to get her feelings out. "I've been planning how I could come back basically from the second my plane touched down at JFK Airport two months ago. An audition came up here in New York for the Royal London Ballet Company and I've been offered a place with them. A prima ballerina position."

"So you'll be living in London?"

"Yes, from the beginning of February. I'm coming home for Christmas and I'll look for a flat near the company then. But I'll want to spend plenty of time in Bowerbridge too, with you, I hope."

"Maybe you could stay with me on weekends when you're not performing . . ."

"I'd love that, if it would be OK?"

"I think that would definitely be OK," said Nathan, pulling her into his arms. "I spent the whole of my flight working out how I was going to convince you to give us a chance."

"What a waste of time." Jessica laughed.

He kissed her, then whispered into her ear, "To return to my original point — I love you, Jessica Stone."

"I love you too, Nathan Townsend."

EPILOGUE

Five years later

Jessica curtseyed and accepted the bouquet of red roses handed to her by the little girl who stared at her with eyes like saucers.

It was the final night of her run as Princess Aurora in *The Sleeping Beauty* at the Royal Opera House. This hadn't been her first principal role, by any means, and it wasn't even the first time she'd played Aurora, but this would be her last role and her final performance.

She'd informed the ballet company directors a month ago, but her retirement wouldn't be officially announced until the following day. She'd wanted to celebrate with her husband first.

Her Substack and Instagram account had been joined by a YouTube channel and had gone from strength to strength as her dance career had, and she was now a regular contributor to several ballet-related websites and magazines. She would continue to write about the ballet world and review ballet performances. She just wouldn't perform anymore.

She looked up into the box she'd reserved for her family. They were all there, standing and clapping for her. Her mum and dad, her brother and Molly, Peter, Emily and Sophie, who both still attended Diana's classes, but much preferred football to ballet. Next to them was Diana herself, and then there was Nathan, her Nathan, clapping harder than anyone else.

They'd lasted only three months with Nathan in Bowerbridge and Jessica in London before Nathan had applied for a position at a GP surgery close to Jessica's dance company. He'd been successful and had decided to rent out his house as an Airbnb and move in with Jessica.

They returned to Bowerbridge regularly, though, staying either in Nathan's house when it was empty or with Jessica's parents, and they never missed one of her nieces or nephew's birthdays and often had them to visit for the weekend to give Andrew and Molly a break.

Jessica had danced for the first three and a half years of their marriage and Nathan had been so supportive, attending every one of her performances that he could.

Now she wanted to start a family with her husband. If there was space for Nathan at the Bowerbridge practice, they would move back there into his house, if not, they'd stay where they were until there was. She wanted to bring her children up close to their grandparents and cousins.

She was ready to retire, and she couldn't wait to celebrate with Nathan later once she was alone with him in their home. She'd had an amazing dancing career, but she was done now. It was her decision and the right time for her, and she had so much to look forward to and to be excited about in the next chapter of her life.

THE END

THE JOFFE BOOKS STORY

We began in 2014 when Jasper agreed to publish his mum's much-rejected romance novel and it became a bestseller.

Since then we've grown into the largest independent publisher in the UK. We're extremely proud to publish some of the very best writers in the world, including Joy Ellis, Faith Martin, Caro Ramsay, Helen Forrester, Simon Brett and Robert Goddard. Everyone at Joffe Books loves reading and we never forget that it all begins with the magic of an author telling a story.

We are proud to publish talented first-time authors, as well as established writers whose books we love introducing to a new generation of readers.

We won Trade Publisher of the Year at the Independent Publishing Awards in 2023. We have been shortlisted for Independent Publisher of the Year at the British Book Awards for the last four years, and were shortlisted for the Diversity and Inclusivity Award at the 2022 Independent Publishing Awards. In 2023 we were shortlisted for Publisher of the Year at the RNA Industry Awards.

We built this company with your help, and we love to hear from you, so please email us about absolutely anything bookish at feedback@joffebooks.com

If you want to receive free books every Friday and hear about all our new releases, join our mailing list: www.joffebooks.com/contact

And when you tell your friends about us, just remember: it's pronounced Joffe as in coffee or toffee!

9 781835 266939